A Caller from Overspace

By the same author

NIGHT OF THE BIG HEAT

THE GIANT STUMBLES

THE GREY ONES

THE COMING OF THE STRANGERS

SWORD ABOVE THE NIGHT

THE SLEEP-EATERS

THE SCREAMING FACE

THE STAR WITCHES

FROOMB!

THE GREEN DRIFT

THE MILLION YEARS TO FRIDAY

THE NOWHERE PLACE

THE YEAR DOT

THE HOLE IN THE WORLD

A SPIDER IN THE BATH

THE LAXHAM HAUNTING

STARSEED ON EYE MOOR

THE WAKING OF THE STONE

A Caller from Overspace

John Lymington

HODDER AND STOUGHTON
LONDON SYDNEY AUCKLAND TORONTO

Lymington, John
A Caller from Overspace.
I. Title
823'.9'1F PR6062.Y53C

ISBN 0 340 23923 9

 Phototypesetting by Rainbow Graphics, Liverpool. Printed in Great Britain for Hodder and Stoughton Limited, Mill Road, Dunton Green, Sevenoaks, Kent, by Lowe & Brydone Printers Limited, Thetford, Norfolk.
Hodder and Stoughton Editorial Office: 47 Bedford Square, London WC1B 3DP

The human philosophy is very difficult to follow. I overheard an Earth man put it as:

"It can't possibly happen to me.

"And if it does, it can't possibly happen twice.

"Can it?"

One

1

BY THE RECKONING of the Earth's activity I estimated the day would have been May 11th when I saw the spaceship lurking behind Saturn, as if resting on the moon belt. It was of a black colour and lit within like an illuminated shark.

Until then I had been enjoying a meditation wandering amid the bubbles and dust of The Accident, watching the hurrying hither and thither; the spinning and circling, with some burning still, others burnt; and all scurrying about as if anxious to get right away from us before it could happen again and they themselves be destroyed.

It helps my philosophy to wander in the cosmic dust and ruminate on failures and the unexpected. Besides, The Old Man had become very tiresome in his claims to have turned a dismal failure into some sort of glorious creation.

In these moments of Grand Illusion he considers making further experiments of a like kind, forgetting that, of the first gas explosion, only the tiniest fraction ever came to anything but drifting hulks. In such moods he is best left to comment on his genius to his long-suffering son, when I may forget what a lousy scientist he is and refresh my spirit with considerations of particles.

I have had many a pleasant time wandering in the spacious outdoors, ruminating on the sparkling of the dying fall-out, for the deeper one goes into the silence of the void the more peaceful becomes the mind.

And then, to disturb me, I spied the spaceship, a grotesque effigy of efficiency, waiting in mischief on the blind side of that little spark which still contains energy in a drifting galaxy of wasted minutiae.

Now I know that there is only one speck which still clings around the Sun which has anything acceptable to offer in the way of living, and that is Earth. For that reason I paid attention and stopped my wanderings to watch the little shark hovering over the moon belt.

Where creatures have evolved from the blow-out, they seem to have developed an animosity towards everything, even themselves. I think perhaps it is a result of their curious belief that they had been created for some definite purpose. Where that idea came from I never could guess.

I remember the last time I visited Earth, my presence was detected by my own carelessness, and the humans immediately jumped to the conclusion that I must be the devil, whoever he may be.

The drifting shark gave obscene birth to a smaller version from its belly; a kind of long-boat from which sailors reach the shore.

I watched this vessel turn from the mother and take

a curving course away, which I could see would lead it directly to Earth once it got on to the light beams which they used at that time for transport over great distances.

Earth is a favourite of mine, because it is the luckiest accident of them all by reason of the magnificent variety of vegetation which has evolved, and the kinds of animals which have come as a result.

Thus, when I saw the shore-boat head for that small place I felt a protective instinct, for visitors between planets often celebrate their arrival by burning everything in sight, whether by accident or not. Not that one can help accidents, as I know too well; but I was apprehensive of the sort which begin by controlled explosions that turn out to be uncontrollable, which is normally the case.

For that reason I returned to earth and the little place where I was before and rested a hundred feet above the top of the church tower. The town was much as I had seen it some two hundred years before; in fact, if I shook the traffic out of it, the whole scene might have been the same.

A fishing town where a few little boats were built on the banks of the Lynn, one of the two rivers which joined at this place and ran in a broad sweep out into the sea.

On the night of May 14th, I saw a solitary ship arrive in the sky and disappear into the sea a mile from the western shore. It had made good time for such a crude machine using a primitive system of light-hopping, as they call it. Even when these accidental creatures travel in the void they still keep their heads firmly sunk into their native earth.

On May 15th, just after dark, an intruder rose up from the water on the sands by Treman Head, and headed, as I could discern, for the vicarage, a fine white house two hundred yards from the church, which had been newly built when last I was here.

I decided that I would wait and see what developed before assuming any protective role. For here was only one, where I had feared hundreds.

Also that one-ness was curious and I watched with increasing interest.

2

On the evening of May 16th, Susan James put her son, Gawain, aged four, to bed at six o'clock. She said Daddy would soon be back and would read him a story before he went to sleep.

She went out and into her bedroom where she looked into a mirror, pushed back her long black hair from obscuring her face, picked a fleck of paint off her nose and said, "My God!" Then she sat down on the wide stool in front of the mirror and thought, "My God!" Then she blew out a long breath and let her chest collapse as much as it could and sighed, "I'm knackered". Which was improbable.

Then she got up, stripped, took some clothes and went along to the bathroom, where the damp bathmat from Gawain's bath was still on the floor, like a rumpled beach, and had a shower. That done, she looked in the steamed mirror on the wall, eyed her black hair hanging like poisonous liana in a rain forest and sticking to her big breasts in weird fingers; she said, "Goosepimples." Then she smiled, draped the string of a broken lamp-pull across her nipples and posed at the mirror.

"I must tell Leo Gawain broke the string," she said, and hung it on the bracket of his shaving mirror in case she forgot.

She spoke to herself quite a bit, and while she dressed in slacks and shirt and commented on the day's work of trying – alone – to paint the vicarage while her husband lolled around his bookshop, flirting with the girls and giving strange urges to present-seeking matrons. It was, of course, an unfair situation, but it gave her a superior hand.

She went down and into the Glory Hole, a room off the main hall, where the living was carried out while the rest of the big house got painted.

The evening meal was ready in the solid-fuel cooker; a splendid stew of practically everything eatable with a faint flavouring of paint, cleverly disguised by the remains of two bottles of Burgundy. Any remains in wine bottles in the vicarage were small.

Susan poured a sherry and sat down to read a magazine all about painting old houses.

At a quarter to seven the front door opened and Arthur Marchant came in, smiling. He threw the folded evening paper across her magazine and kissed her.

"Hallo, Shagbag, the dearest," he said. "Ah, the sherry's out, I see. Good."

She sat back and screwed her head round to see him.

"Leo's late," she said.

"Let's nip quickly up on the bed," he said.

She looked at him steadily.

"Where have you been?" she said.

"I've been with Elfrida," he said. "You know how she rouses me." He sat on the coffee table opposite her. "Do you know what she was doing? I see you don't. She was trying to pick pennies up off the corner of a table with her person."

"What?"

"There were pennies all over the floor. She saw a negress doing it in Madagascar."

"I don't believe it. Not even of Elfrida. What did you go there for?"

"She's helping me about the church."

"Oh, she is, is she?"

"Damn! You're not jealous, are you? We're divorced, remember."

"I have my natural feelings still. One doesn't sell those with the package."

"Well, if that's all there still, why not hop up on the bed? A few minutes."

"It's not that I'm worried about morals or legalities."

"And I should think not."

"I have been painting all day. I need to relax, not get all active. And supper's ready. Where is Leo?"

"Why do you call him that? His name's Leofric." He drank some sherry. "I'm having a bit of shindy about the church."

"Because you've bought it? Well, the people who never went to church are always upset when it gets sold, aren't they? You're bound to get that. I told you. We all told you."

"Well, this isn't actually about buying it. It's what I want to do with it."

She tossed the magazine on the seat beside her and sat back.

"Well, that was bound to happen, wasn't it? I suppose they've seen the stuff being taken in there?"

"There are a lot of nosey parkers, you know. The odd goat's head showing up under the wraps. 'What's that?' they say. 'Is it going to be a natural history museum?' you know."

"And when they do know - bang! You'll have to run. To be honest, I've felt uneasy about it myself. I begin to wonder if the Old Gentleman himself won't come down for the opening."

"That would be a Big Sale," said Arthur. "If only he could be persuaded. But there—" He sighed.

"I wish Leo would come," Susan said. "Gaw's asleep by now."

"You bet?"

"He's been terribly busy all day. Daddy gave him a box of plasticine and he's been in the nursery doing nothing else but sticking lumps of the stuff together in weird shapes."

"That could sell. Think of Elfrida. She was in the garden doing a rain dance for her cucumbers. Painted all over, she was."

"I thought you said she was—"

"This was yesterday when I got that magic mirror from her."

"You went yesterday as well?" She had sat forward, now sat back. "Sorry. It's habit."

"Of course. That's why I keep suggesting— That sounds like him now. Leo?"

Leo James came in carrying two new books and an umbrella. He kissed Susan.

"Where's Rowena?" Arthur said.

"She's gone flying." Leo went to the drinks cupboard. "I'm parched. Do you know what? That lunatic Elfrida turned up at near closing time and wanted to know how her book's doing. She'd got a bloody great cushion tied to her belly to look pregnant. She gets first on the bus like that, she said."

"Go and say good night to Gaw," said Susan. "He's waiting."

Leo drank half a glass of beer, then nodded and went upstairs. He was not long gone and came back holding something behind his back.

"He's asleep," he said. "Morpheus, in the arms of."

"What have you got behind you?" Susan said. "I can tell by that fat-headed grin you've got something. Show!"

"Plasticine," Leo said.

"Well? He played with it all day. Wouldn't speak, hardly. It's not stuck all over the carpet, is it?"

"Nothing at all like that, Sue. Not a bit."

Arthur watched in silence. He sensed something odd and, clearly, Sue did, too. She sat forward sharply.

"What is it?" she said.

"Look what the boy made," said Leo. He cleared a place on the table then set a six-inch clay figure on it.

"He had it on his pillow instead of teddy. I put teddy there as usual."

"He made – made that?" she said, unbelieving. "He couldn't have. It's – it's so sexy. He's only four!"

"Oh that's natural," said Leo, shrugging. "I mean, as soon as one's born one is plugged into the jolly titty, and the idea becomes fixed in the head. It impregnates the Id."

"But these are enormous and points like spikes. And that's not the lot, darling. I mean, the whole thing is exaggerated."

"Well, perhaps that's what he sees, in his artistic view, that is. I mean, Picasso drew them with one tit or three, whatever the poor lass looked like to him."

Susan stared at it with a very puzzled look, then shook her head.

"He couldn't have done it. Somebody is playing a joke!" She looked at Arthur.

"Not me, sweetie. I didn't come in till you saw me and I didn't go upstairs first." He did not take his eyes from the figure to speak. He seemed fascinated. "Sue, have you got your instant camera? The one that shoots and then offers the scene like a toilet roll."

"Why?"

"I wish for it to record this strange affair. It's very important. Please. And a ruler, or a tape measure."

"He's off on a down beat," said Sue. "It's over there somewhere. Probably in the waste basket. The camera. It was on that shelf but isn't now."

Arthur got up and looked. Leo looked at him, then at Sue, then at the figure.

"It's Elfrida," Leo said, with a grin.

"Not even Elfrida looks like that," said Sue.

"You haven't seen her rain dance," said Arthur, and came back with the camera. "Ruler?"

"We use the edge of this old road book. It's marked, you see? For maps."

"Genius. But it doesn't start where it stands, does it. Never mind. Move the model to the edge of the table, then hold the book so the begin line on the scale comes at the table level."

Susan obeyed and said, "But what's this for?"

Arthur sighted the camera. "It's important." He clicked. He took four pictures, moving the figure round for a different view for each.

"You're not thinking of the Royal Academy, are you?" Susan said.

"I'm not thinking of that." Arthur laid out the prints on the edge of the table. "Now, that's just it. Take that model, stick it up on that high mantelpiece and don't touch it. I am aglow with inspiration."

He gathered up the pictures, took Leo's evening paper and folded them in that, then went out into the hall.

"Where the hell are you going?" Leo said.

"To Elfrida," said Arthur.

"What?" said Susan. "What for? That is, how long for?"

"Couple of hours, sweetie. Keep mine in the oven."

Susan looked at Leo. Leo looked back. Leo moved, took up the figure, looked at it, then put it on the high mantelpiece. Both looked at it.

"It's odd, you know," Leo said. "I don't quite see how you could do that with fingers."

Susan walked to the mantelpiece and, for the first time, took a close look at the figure.

"You're right. It looks like a tool. But Gaw can't use a tool!" She looked at Leo. "I suppose it is the stuff you gave him, is it?"

"I suppose you didn't do it, Sue?"

"Can you imagine me doing that?" She pointed.

"As an ironic comment - aha."

"On Elfrida?"

"She'd love it. Wait. I'll look in the playroom and make sure it's Gaw's stuff. I'm sure, because the usual kids' box is all colours, and the only stuff I could get was mono. But I'll look."

"I'll tip out the grub. I'm hungry. I've been painting all day."

"Darling!" He threw her on the sofa and kissed her with embellishments and she began laughing and then pushed him off.

"I'm tired," she said.

"You didn't feel like it, but paint effect is hard to assess." He looked at the figure again. "I'm damned if I know, but I'll just make sure."

He went out and ran up the fine, uncarpeted staircase, wide enough to drive a car down if you had that kind of film in mind.

Susan went and lifted the stew out of the oven. The scrubbed wooden top of the kitchen table was big enough to sleep four. Adorned with Arthur's antique Queen Anne china, his Georgian silver, vast wooden peppermills and Victorian salt cellar, cherubs and all, it looked as if the still life was much of an age, and all

Susan needed was a big bell skirt, low cut neckline and mob cap to fit the surround.

Leo came down.

"Yes. It's the stuff all right. Most of it's gone, but odd lumps are lying about. They look like Gaw's work. And one doughnut man, one leg, two short arms, one nose on chin and three eyes, or perhaps its an ear mixed up. Picasso, all over again."

She came out of the kitchen and looked at the figure again.

"Nobody came today, you know," she said. "I mean, I was the only one in the house with him. Took him for a walk, of course, and he didn't want to play out in his wigwam. I just thought he was hooked on the clay stuff."

Leo put his arm round her.

"Why are you worried?"

She looked at him curiously.

"Aren't you?"

"Well, it's odd. But you do have young geniuses. It could have happened."

They both stared at the model.

"It looks a bit like those primitive idols," she said. "You know the sort of thing. Fertility idols. Things like that."

"Yes. It's odd to think somebody else might have got up there and done it. But he would have said so, wouldn't he? He would have been scared of a stranger anyhow, and the way he's sleeping now, with the great smile of the true artist spread across his chops, he couldn't be scared."

"His chops? That dear, cherubic little face – his

chops?" She pushed him away. "You are inelegant."

"Remember, I am the son of a Saxon yeoman. Remember Athelstaneham and sink the *Bismarck*. Chops is a term of cherubic endearment to us."

"Like manure. Shall we begin or wait for Arthur?"

"Not if he's gone to Elfrida. They're probably rolling in the aisles yet."

"Vulgarity, Saxonity, bloody shovelry. Remember, I am the daughter of a gentleman vicar."

"Very well, then. Angelic chops. Let's have the grub."

They went into the kitchen. He watched while she ladled stew out of the earthenware pot.

"As you say, it is odd," he said. "And then Arthur zooming off like that. What did he think it was? Black magic symbolism?"

"Arthur is inclined to zoom in sharp zigzags like a blue-arsed fly. You know that."

"Yes, but Elfrida's a soul mate as far as that's concerned. They're both soused in anything. He just likes to watch other people drown themselves."

"That's not very kind to your other husband. What stew is this, sweetheart?"

"Wallpaper," she said. "Is it done enough?"

"Just a dash too much paste," he said. "Otherwise, superb, a glutton's piece of resistance." He cocked his head. "That's the church clock! Has he got it going again?"

"It's chimed today, come to think of it. I suppose he has. He didn't say." She got up suddenly and went out into the hall. She stayed a moment, then came back. "I thought I heard Gaw out of bed."

"My dear, the creaks and groans in this place sound like the entire contents of the graveyard out of bed."

"I am not entirely in favour of your jokes about the graveyard," she said. "Not when its practically on the doorstep."

"Forgive me. By the way we had a rep in today flogging a new list, and do you know what? There's a new one entitled *Thoughts in a Graveyard.* I said, 'What about Gray?' That shook him. He'd forgotten."

"Who's Gray?"

"My dear punitive expedition, he wrote an Elegy in the churchyard at Stoke Poges by the Thames. 'The lowing herd winds slowly o'er the lea—' "

"Of course, of course, of course," she said.

" 'And leaves the world to darkness, and to me.' Finest last line in any language put in as starters. It always worried me. Do you know that bloody clock's striking again?"

"I can hear it."

Both looked to the window. It was nearly dark outside, but the straight pillar of the church tower stood clear against the dying glow of day over the sea.

"It's out of hand," Leo said. "Didn't like being startled out of its sleep."

"Supposing it hasn't been wound up?" she said, still looking out.

He started. "Don't say things like that! What's the matter? Gone fey? If it hadn't been wound it wouldn't go dong, would it? Or would it? You're beginning to give me the faint shakies."

"I'm sorry. It's that model thing. It gives me an odd sort of feeling."

"Intuitive shivers," he said. "I still think he did it himself, somehow."

"He couldn't possibly have done it with his little fingers. It's some kind of tool."

"A teaspoon handle," he said helpfully. "Of course!"

She got up and went through into the Glory Hole. She looked at the figure again. He watched her through the open doorway.

"Do you know what it looks like to me?" she said. She came back and put a hand on his shoulder. "Don't think I'm being too silly, but it looks as if it was done with a claw, a blunt claw."

"My dear pussycat! What tigers go round nurseries amusing the kiddies like that?"

"Tigers!" She took her hand away. "You have a nightmare mind! I *am* his mother, you know! Tigers! Ergh! I think I've gone all cold."

"My dear girl! It was you who said claw, and what comes after claw? Tigers, lions, eagles, vultures— No! not vultures! I was thinking of those other things, honestly. Doves. That was it."

Saved by the crash of the front door opening too wide, he looked at his watch.

"Where's the lights? What is this? Ghost-baiting night or something? Hang on, Elfrida. Hold fast."

"He's brought her back," said Susan, shortly.

"I hope she's got rid of that cushion. I felt guilty."

"An association of evil ideas," Susan said and went into the Glory Hole as Elfrida and Arthur came in through the other door.

Elfrida was thirty-five, of medium height, good legs,

bottom, waist and then a bosom of aggressive splendour; Susan said it must be forty-eight. Her face was almost ugly but always bright-eyed with zest and instant glee.

"My pretty one, how are you?" she said, kissing Susan. "My, you look enchanting, even in that lot, dear. And how's the noble knight? Fast asleep? Good. Good for him and everybody else, I imagine." She laughed.

"Have you eaten? Would you like some stew?" said Susan.

"No; yes," said Elfrida. "Why, there's Leo lurking in there. Hail, Caesar! It's all right. I jettisoned the cushion. He was so embarrassed, dear, you'd never believe," she told Susan.

They all sat down and ate stew.

"Is that all right?" said Susan.

"Excellent, dear," said Elfrida, bringing a flask from her handbag. "All it needs is a dash of Scotch. Allow me."

She poured a slosh on everybody's, ending with her own.

"You're right," said Leo. "It makes it." He smiled at Susan. "Not that it wasn't beautiful before, and I *have* had most of it."

She smiled back. It cut him.

"Arthur, the books and the effigy, please. The light is good in here." Elfrida began to eat with determination. That not being enough, she used a spoon instead of a knife and shovelled it down.

"It's wallpaper," said Leo, smiling at her.

"And bloody good wallpaper," said Elfrida.

Arthur went out and got the figure and books. He put the books at her left hand and stood the figure on a cleared space in front of her.

When she saw it, she stopped eating. She put a hand in her great bag and pulled out a pair of heavy horn rims. She put them on and looked again at the impertinent womanette.

She pushed her plate aside nearly into Arthur's lap, and replaced it with the books.

Pages flipped, streaming past her fingers. She knew where to look, and how to flick book pages.

While they watched her the church clock struck again.

Susan looked at Arthur. "That's your clock," she said, staring hard. "Did you have it started?"

Arthur cocked his head. "In the church tower? No. Perhaps something slipped."

"It *keeps on* striking," said Susan staring harder as if to make him uneasy. "If it goes on irregularly you won't sleep. You know what you are with irregular noises at night."

"You look as if you're going to laugh," Arthur said.

Elfrida began to talk as she riffled pages, holding a finger in one gap, another in another, in a third she put a biscuit. A second biscuit she ate.

"You say the young knight made this?"

"Leo gave him the plasticine at nine this morning in the nursery," said Susan. "Gawain then refused to leave the damned room. He kicked up a fuss when I took him for a walk and was back up there again as soon as we got in. At first I was grateful, and then I began to think it was odd. I called him for tea, but he just yelled back to let us have it up there. So I took it up there."

"What did you see up there?" said Elfrida, sitting back with one arm forward, three fingers still separating pages.

"A mess as usual. And balls of plasticine scattered round."

"I mean you didn't see *Sexmädchen*?"

"Of course not. It would have knocked me. It does now."

"It could have been there though, hidden?"

"Why would he hide anything from me?"

"Children do, dear. They don't want to share everything with Mummy, hurtful though it may be."

"I understand about children. He's mine."

"Woman's hour," said Leo quietly. "Sit back till the bell goes."

"And you can shut up," said Susan. "I'm worried about this."

"So am I, you trout. A genius in the family is always an unexpected expense."

"Right," said Elfrida like a sergeant-major commanding hush. "Now let's look at these pictures. Gather round. I'll show you six."

They gathered round behind her. She showed them six, one after the other, putting a biscuit in each place, then got up.

"There they are. Compare them with the *Sexmädchen*."

She went to look out at the church tower, taking her bag from which she snatched a thin cigar.

"Does that clock know anything about the time, or is

it a bell-ringing contest?" she said, slowly blowing smoke.

"This can't be!" said Susan, looking up at her.

Elfrida turned to the table.

"Surely it has to be. This model is an exact reproduction from the photographs, described as Plate Forty-eight and so on. Well, I'll tell you what you find if you read the flatulent script. That is a figure found in Peru, and at present in a private museum there. It was discovered by diggings at a place where scientists thought were some remains of space visitors of very ancient times. Anyhow, the figure has been a puzzle ever since it was found forty years ago. The age is reckoned at about seven thousand years. The clay it is made from is not known on this earth.

"So upstairs, made from what is obviously modern commercial plasticine, we are suddenly presented with an absolute replica of that figure which is at present in Peru, however many miles that is—"

"Cut the paraphrase," said Leo. "You mean this model's exactly the same as some space pilot's doodle, who did it in his vehicle seven thousand years ago from stuff he brought from home, wherever that was?"

"I mean that."

"Have you found any other things like this - alien things - in your travels, Elfie?" said Arthur.

"Elfie! Does she *look* Elfie?" Susan said to Leo's ear. "I ask you!"

"You ask me what, dear?" said Elfrida.

"Just what Arthur's asking."

"There were some odd sods and bits in Egypt and around Ararat, which is really a commercial for insurance against flood. No. Not anything like this. And according to the books I have – I haven't got them all (and I regret that deeply) by a long chalk – conduct me, Leo. Where was I when the lights changed?"

"The books you have. That's what you were saying."

"According to the books I have, yes. I remember. But I have now forgotten what I was going to say." She looked out of the window. "What happened to my rain dance? There's going to be a drought."

"It's all in Spanish or something," Susan said, looking up at her.

"Certainly. Published in Brazil or some such. I don't think it ever came out anywhere but in South America. I brought a dictionary. It's underneath."

"No, thanks," Susan turned to the hall. "Come upstairs with me, Leo. I just want to look around."

"Hell! you don't think somebody's up there, do you?" Leo said.

"Take the shillelagh," said Arthur, generously, and watched them go into the hall. "Well, Elf. What do you make of it?"

"I make a bit of a cold shiver out of it, but that's because I'm not thinking logically. It seems fact that this replica was made today with stuff that only came into the house last night, according to Leo. It wasn't done before nine a.m. because that's when he gave the full box to the offspring. Susan said nobody came today.

"Somebody made an almost exact replica of something last made seven thousand years adrift, and nobody is here to do it unless it was Susan."

"Would she? She was too taken aback when she saw it. Somebody might have got in up there. It's a big place."

"As a mother Susan is a Grade A fusspot, one ear pricked all the time. She would be unconsciously listening. But then, children do talk to themselves and croon, of course. I remember I used to have a friend who wasn't there – her hair was a terrible mess and I used to reprimand her; it was fair and had jam on it sometimes— On what? I have forgotten. Was it toast? Oh no, hair. I think I must have left a bracket open somewhere and my thoughts got away."

"The trouble is, Elfie, you're too excited to think," said Arthur slowly.

She looked at the figure. "Ah," she sighed. "Perhaps, yes." She sat down and looked harder. "I just don't understand. Seven thousand years, it's reckoned—"

"Well, that isn't long, is it?"

"Not historically. Personally it's a hell of a time. There's one in Peru. Here's one exactly the same to all intents and purposes, made here some time this afternoon."

"You don't think the boy's – odd, perhaps?"

"Become possessed, do you mean? For heaven's sake don't suggest it in front of Sue!"

"I may be a lot of things but plain daft isn't one. She's jolted. Do I think he is with a devil? I haven't seen him for weeks. How could I tell without?"

She examined the figure closely, then shook her head.

"In the book it says that one of the puzzles is what

sort of tool was used to fashion it. Fingers couldn't do it. But what sort of tool? All sorts were tried, a number of artists and sculptors had a go and couldn't reproduce it exactly, the finish that is. A sort of adzed surface or beaten copper or God knows." She sat back. "Well, whatever it was it's here again, done this afternoon in the nursery."

"And the original was alien," Arthur said. "Altogether alien. Alien material, type of carving, finish, and, of course, general artistic form. As if the chap had never seen a female figure before and was inspired by its relevance."

"That was the theory of a few years back. That the aliens came and podded the local females, then went back into the skies to die."

"Leaving what in the maternity units?"

"Well, intelligent humans, I suppose."

"What happened to them?" asked Arthur, and went to find the scotch.

Two

1

"I didn't tidy up when he went to bed," Susan said.

They stood looking round the playroom, watched by the silent button eyes of Teddies, Snoopies, Kermits; all suddenly become like real things, strange things, like evil gnomes in legends of inevitable retribution.

"It isn't worth tidying every time," Leo said and went to the windows. They were locked as usual. It was a long way to the ground from there.

A sudden rumble and rushing sound starting up made them jump, then Susan relaxed.

"It's that air-conditioner thing. It must have come on."

"It's a waste of juice at night," he said, and switched it off. Then he thought of something. "Why did it come on?"

"The switch is a bit dickey. I was going to tell you. You have to make sure it's off."

He made sure. They looked around again.

"Oh and the cord on the bathroom light's broken

off. You have to reach up and pull the thing down."

"We shall all electrocute ourselves one of these days," he said. "Anyway, nobody could have got in here without you seeing them coming up the stairs, unless they used the other stairs in the flat next door."

"The landing door's locked to stop Gaw getting in there. Arthur's got some fine stuff in there now, all stacked around."

"Well, then nobody got up here. QED."

"Oh, and the lock on the landing door needs something. It won't undo."

"And I suppose the bath's fallen through the floor. Never mind, it'll do for a sink downstairs."

"I'm going to look at him."

They went very quietly and looked into the nursery. In the dim nightlight by the bed they saw the child sleeping and smiling at some pleasant dream.

"That is not a worried child," said Leo.

She shook her head. "No. But I'm a puzzled Mum."

They closed the door and stood together on the landing, looking into the great hall. It was very quiet.

"There must have been somebody in the nursery with him," she said. "He just couldn't have done that. You don't think the place is haunted?"

He put his arm round her waist and held her tight.

"I think it isn't places that are haunted, but people. And if Sir Gawain spent the afternoon with a ghost, he certainly wasn't frightened of it. In fact, it was a ghost he made up himself, so it's his secret."

"And his secret invention made that nymph? Come off it, bucket!"

"Bucket?" he said as they went down the wide stairs. "What's this?"

"Paint buckets," she said. "I hate them."

When they got to the bottom Elfrida was standing at the kitchen doorway. Arthur was behind her by the table, drinking scotch.

"And all was peaceful and calm as usual," said Elfrida, and cocked her head. "You and Ro are such beautiful big girls you should have gone into the Bluebell chorus."

"We tried. That's how we met," said Susan. "On the battlefield of Adelphi, struggling amidst the bare bubbling breasts of a field of Bluebells."

"Why battlefield?" said Elfrida. "Catwise, do you mean?"

"Lord, no. Fatherwise. He turned up, having heard what I intended, complete with square top bowler, ecclesiastical waistcoat and riding crop. He walloped my bum, so I didn't go further. Ro had got turned down so she came with me. It was the first time we met."

"Your father is narrow-minded?"

"Not a bit. His one regret about Sodom and Gomorrah was that he was born too late to be there. It's just that some fathers get jealous of their daughters— Where is Ro?"

"I suppose she's still flying," said Leo. "Probably landed somewhere. Lost as usual. She can read a map but doesn't know left from right, port from starboard or arse from face when it comes to orientating."

"Why did you teach her for God's sake?" said Arthur, coming out with his glass.

"She threatened to withdraw connubial joys."

"I found that a loser with my husband," said Elfrida. "He seemed relieved, so I changed my ploy to demanding it twice as often and he just had to give in over whatever it was."

"I didn't know you were married?" said Susan.

"Divorced. He claimed I embarrassed him and lost him business."

"Embarrassed him?" said Arthur.

"Well, one thing rather upset the whole balance was when I decided to make a sensation at the chairman's annual party. I went topless."

"I see," said Arthur. "Surely that was popular?"

"No. It's my twisted sense of amusing people, I suppose. I painted red triangles on my nipples and wrote Draught Bass on my belly and Reg was enraged. However, I went home with the chairman. In fact, I couldn't get rid of the chairman. Reg got more and more strained and finally - bust! It was all a misunderstanding, really. I was only twenty-four—"

She stopped and stared at the wall above the staircase. She took her glasses off, shook her head and looked again.

"What's the matter?" Susan said sharply.

"I thought I saw a shadow on the wall up there, like somebody going upstairs. It's these new glasses. Lovely for the close look but they give the most odd dimensions in distance."

"Going upstairs—?" Susan put a hand to her mouth, then took it away, said a rude word and ran.

"It's me! These glasses!" Elfrida called after her,

and then lowered the volume. "Oh Christ, I shouldn't have said that."

Leo looked up at his wife.

"It's her glasses! She said so!"

Susan ran on. "I'm going to stay up here a while."

"Oh God," said Leo.

"What happened about the chairman?" said Arthur, coming back to realities.

"The chairman? Oh, him! Well Reg went and rowed with him and resigned. Then, when it got round, the chairman's wife came round and commiserated with Reg out of spite, but I didn't marry Reg because he wasn't good for women and when I came home at four one afternoon they were having a bath together so I went for my tour of the rain forests of Sumatra where I found that extraordinary—"

The phone rang in the Glory Hole.

"Who's that?" said Arthur.

"How the hell do I know?" said Leo. "Answer the bloody thing. It's Ro, I expect. She's landed somewhere."

Arthur took his glass with him.

"Was there a shadow up on that wall, Elfrida?" Leo said quietly.

"Yes. Like I said."

"Sue's just got a notion the place might be haunted."

"It never was before. I knew this place. I came here before you. When it was a vicarage and Parson Fragg had it. You should have seen his whiskers. Why do people grow whiskers? He looked like an owl in a bush." Have you seen that bush over by the graveyard? Bushy whiskers tickle, of course, but why a parson?" She looked at the ceiling. "I've lost a bracket again. Where was I? Oh, yes! But then, no. Why whiskers?"

"Parson Fragg!" he said shortly.

"He had some items from Africa. Very weird. I kept sucking up socially, you know, jumbles, bumbles, tombolas, boltombas - where did they get bingo? - well, anyway, it wasn't haunted then. I always ask about things like that. These old places— He's a long time on the blower, is he not?"

As if instructed there was a sharp ding from the room and Arthur came out.

"Bloody woman," he said, blankly.

"Ro?" said Leo.

"No. Bitch anonymous. You've never heard such foul stuff. Talk about the Cardinal's curse. Not in it. Every part of me was going to rot and drop off, specially my balls. Three times she said that."

"About the church?" said Elfrida sharply.

"Yes. It's got out. I don't know who blew it but that crone knew. Hell." He turned round and sat on the stairs.

"Unpleasant," said Leo. "But you'll get over it." He looked up to the landing rails. "Are you all right, Sue?"

"I'm in the bathroom. Here. Come up a minute."

Leo bounded up the stairs almost treading on Arthur in his sudden alarm. When he got into the bathroom Sue had the window open.

"What's that?" she said, pointing upwards.

He joined her at the window and looked up into the quiet sky.

"A sort of a glow," he said. "What is it?"

"It's too fuzzy to see. Is it a UFO or something? I mean, they're not plane lights. It's a clear night. Look at the stars."

They stared up in silence for a minute, Leo leaning farther and farther out until she grabbed his jacket to pull him back.

"We're at the wrong angle," he said. "I think it's over the church. Let's try our bedroom."

They hurried along the landing.

"What's the matter?" Arthur yelled up.

"Hang on," Leo called back.

From the bedroom window the glow itself was less noticeable but its position was clearly above the church tower.

"I think its the town lights reflecting on some smoke or mist," Leo said.

The others came audibly up the uncarpeted stairs, disturbed by one unusual matter after the other. Arthur went into the bedroom, Elfrida following. The lights were off but the glow of town lights beyond the church was enough to make obstacles clear.

"What is it?" Elfrida said. "My God! That clock's clanking again! There must be some boy got in the tower. It couldn't do that on its own, surely?"

They all leant out of the windows and looked up into the sky above the church tower.

"It's a smoke ring," said Elfrida, definitely. "It's catching the light." She straightened and looked at her watch. "It just clanks away any old time. You ought to see if a boy's got in there, Arthur."

"My God, yes!" he said, suddenly. "The insurance! And suppose he kills himself! That would be bad for business!"

He turned from the window.

"Can I come with you?" Elfrida said. "I haven't seen inside yet."

"What's the rush?" Leo said. "That clock's been doing that for hours now."

When Arthur and Elfrida went out the moon was rising, and the smoke ring was fading with the new light increasing in the sky above it. They crossed the circle of the drive and opened the iron gate into the garden and graveyard. The path down between the old, lurching stones was clear in the growing moonlight. At the end four stone steps led down into the forecourt of the church. The heavy oak doors were still locked. Arthur turned towards the tower.

"There's a separate door into the tower for the bell-ringers." He turned and began to walk fast. She kept pace.

"Are the bells still up there?"

"No. They went over to the new church, five or six years back. It's just the clock clanger that's left. As you can hear, it's a little bit cracked."

They came to the tower door. That, too, was locked. He looked up to the apex of the roof where the tower butted against it.

"If a kid climbed up there he must have scared himself," he said.

"It could be done. Open the bloody door. I'm agog."

He used his keys. They went into the tower. He fumbled for a lantern on a shelf right of the doorway. When he had it he shone the long beam right up through the great hole in the middle of the tower floor, on to the bell beams and the dull gears of the clock in a cage seventy feet up.

"No one's there," he said, relieved.

"Well, the clock isn't going, is it?"

He watched for a few seconds. "No."

"Then what rang the bell?"

"All I can think of is that Samuel Goffin, Esquire is sleepwalking."

"Who's he?"

"He's the chap who died in 1782. His stone reels against the gate as you come in. One day, he'll collapse and block up that gate."

They were about to turn and go out when there was a clack and a sudden whirr from high above. They stopped. Arthur flashed the beam up to the mechanism again.

A hammer clanked the bell four times, at irregular intervals, then stopped and left the echoes to chase each other up into the top of the tower and out of the louvres to fly away over the town roofs.

"There must be a fault," he said.

"You haven't got a ruddy *ghost* up there, have you?"

"I don't know and I'm not going to look in the dark. I'll have the clock looked at tomorrow."

They went out again. The moon was growing bright.

"How long is it since the church was actually used?" Elfrida asked. She stopped and looked back up at the tower, then along the line of the roof.

"Seventeen years."

"I think it's a pity to sell churches, but there you are."

"They had too many. Three, but could only manage two. For years the rector here just stayed in the vicarage and wouldn't budge. Under the old livings you couldn't get rid of the incumbent. He killed the place. Wouldn't do anything. The more they tried to push him out the tighter he stuck.

"Finally they cut this one out and used the other two churches. There was an acceptable priest over in the bigger town who was given both.

"The old man finally died in the vicarage. By then the new church, only built in 1813, had got all the business and when the death happened, both church and vicarage needed a lot of repairs. The house was repaired and used as a retired priests' rest home for a while, until it was decided to sell up and take the money for church funds.

"By that time it would have cost too much to bring this church back into proper order and so it stood while they made up their minds.

"Structural repairs were done, but without any fussy bits. No replacement gargoyles or such. Finally, once churches began to be sold, they decided to flog this one. I was the mug."

"You'll get a very weird public section for customers."

"So long as they pay," he shrugged, "and they will, I promise."

The clock struck again.

"It's very strange, that," she said.

"Obviously," he said firmly and carefully, "it's something mechanical. Let's go back, or do you wish for a romp on a grassy grave?"

"Oh, sir! You are too kind. But no. Not on a grassy grave. I'd get wet."

"We'd have a halo over us," he said and started laughing.

She looked up above the tower. The ring of light was still there, but very high and small, as if about to penetrate the roof of the world and disappear.

"That's no smoke ring," she said.

"Don't argue with me. I never said it was."

2

Rowena was very beautiful. Even the girls who are turned down by Bluebell are taller, fuller, more beautiful than most. So when she, lost in her practice flight and in darkness, made a muck of one thing more and found a Royal Air Force field, on the eastern side of the estuary, suddenly lit up for the commencement of night-flying by jets which were running up for take-off she struck lucky.

She taxied in to the lights of the control tower, running up over the grass and bursting a tyre on the small, one-foot posts and chains protecting the rose beds.

When an airman opened the door and looked in,

momentarily at a loss to describe such crass behaviour, he was arrested by her beauty in all directions. As she took off the ear-phones, which she had not switched on, she said, huskily, "I'm lost."

His grin spread ultra white. "I'll find you," he said. and gave her a hand.

By the time the hospitality of the service was really getting going in the mess, the visiting Air Vice Marshal thought it time to take her to the home and husband she had mentioned three times but had not rung once.

She kissed three officers before she went because, as she explained, "I might have been dead without."

"Without what, in particular?" asked the Air Vice Marshal, as he shut her in his car.

"Kindness in letting me come down," she said.

"It was done for the safety of our aircraft and because you would not answer any signals, so we knew it was a twit of fate suspended above us."

"A twit?" she asked stiffly.

"Correct. You had forgotten to activate your radio."

"I was only having local practice. It wasn't necessary."

"How local is local? The airfield you left was fifty miles from here. This is a small country. Jets are very fast. They need to know where everybody is on practice nights."

"Don't make such a fuss," she said, unbending. "I didn't mean it, really."

They both laughed. The road was quiet. The car was quiet. The officer was in no hurry.

"Have you been married long?" he asked, pleasantly.

"Well, do you mean both times added together?"

"You've been married twice?"

"Fate. Nothing but. My husband put a bun in my best friend's oven. Then we decided to swop legally instead of every other night, sort of thing."

He started to laugh, then calmed and said, "It sounds intriguing. Do tell me."

"Well, you see, how it happened was this—" She stayed looking at the road with her mouth open, shying at the hedge, not sure which foot should go first. "Well, we were two girls, very beautiful, of course, nothing to choose - that sort of thing. And we met these two boys and we were all very fond of each other all the way round, a sort of permutation, you know, A and B, B and C, C and D, D and A— am I all right so far?"

"A sort of equal opportunities harem?"

She laughed, and then sobered. "What size were those gins?"

"Average mess size for visiting pretty ladies. Do go on."

"It wasn't facetious at all, " she said. "But we got into business together, you see? Our own business; books, antiques, dealing, wheeling, whatever. And I married Leo, who runs the books, and Sue married Arthur, who buys, wheels, deals and flops around while I run the antiques *sales*. I actually get the money he spends— They seem to have been very large gins."

"You don't feel ill?"

"No. I feel I want some more."

"We'll arrange it. What happened next? You got married."

"Well, we were all very pleased about it!"

"You mean ACDBDACB, and so on?"

"Of course. But when the little one got planted we all thought it best to change partners so the lad could be legitimate. You see, it's all right being a bastard if you're rich, but it can be unfunny if you're not."

"Old customs die hard," he agreed.

"I don't think they die at all. There's an industry which pretends they do, but pretending gets found out. Sometimes I think if somebody came back on earth after two or three hundred years, he wouldn't find the people any different."

"I'm sure he wouldn't. We seem to be getting near your town. I am rather hungry. I wonder if there's a good pub somewhere handy, preferably before I drop you off."

"Of course. I'll tell you when."

"You divorced and remarried to protect the child?"

"Of course. That was the proper thing."

"But how did you know?"

"There was an infallible pointer," she said. "Arthur was always telling people they were grumpy as a bear with a sore cock. Well, it boomeranged. He stuck his picnic gadget in a poisonous thorn bush while peeing in the dark one night— Do you know, I think I'd better have another drink to get sober. I am speaking in the most inelegant manner."

"It's charming, I assure you. Well?"

"Anyhow, he injured his piece, and it festered and

was awful for two months and that's when Gawain was sown. So there's no doubt, you see."

"Of course," said the Air Vice Marshal drily. "We are coming up to the town. Where's the pub?"

"Just past these lights then into that gap over there on the left," she said, pointing.

"Right?" he queried.

"Right, it is. Sorry. I didn't think straight."

He drove into the car park behind the pub and parked by a barn which backed on to the church grounds. As they got out he looked up to the now faint glow in the sky over the tower.

"It's still there, I see. That glow. See it? It was bright earlier. We had a go tracking it. Testing equipment earlier this evening. Radar, infra red, laser - never got any signal at all, not even of light."

"It's probably something reflecting off something."

He laughed. "But I said we didn't even track any light."

"Of course. Now let me introduce you to the Eater's Arms. You mustn't mention frozen food or tinned things or anything. He goes down to the boats every morning and selects his fish. His meat comes from a certain farm and he hangs it till it's ready; his fruit and veg come from a special nurseryman who keeps horses. Oh boy! It's a fuss. But it is gorgeous food." She sighed. "I'm hungry."

While they ate grilled sole she said, "We bought the church behind here. Or the company did. We're the company. James, Marchant and Wives Limited. It makes a change, perhaps? It's fun, too, because most people don't notice the comma and say, 'Wives?

What? How many's he got?' And they come in to find out. And usually they buy something. Arthur – that's my present one – thinks of things like that."

"You all live together?"

"No. The house is divided. There's a flat the other end with a door in between."

They were in the bar. A number of other eaters were at tables laid mostly near the walls. The bar itself was busy. At the end of the meal, they sat back.

"I can't help noticing," he said, "certain people in this bar have been eyeing you with hostility. Is that to do with having bought the church?"

"That's very astute of you. Very acute. Yes. It's been closed donkey's years but when vurriners buys summat 'bout yur, it gets right up their little noses."

"You're foreigners? Where's your shop, then?"

"Well, you know Barnstaple?"

"Not really, no."

"I thought you were CO at the station."

"Oh, no. I'm down from Defence."

"Oh, I see. Top brassy. Well, I think you're nice. My father was in the Air Force, but now he's a broker. Gets broker all the time. Oh, God! Are you sure that mess gin was genuine? I never say things like that unless I'm a bit tiddly."

"It's the relief from having been lost in the dark all by yourself," he said. "One expands with gratitude to the Almighty and all his grace, and in the excitement one gin counts like four."

He looked round.

"Do they put people up here?" he said.

"I thought you were going back to the station."

"I could, but I'm flying back to London from St. Mawgan in the morning. That's in the other direction."

"I think I flew over it this evening," she said, thoughtfully.

"You probably did," he said, gently. "London as well, I shouldn't wonder."

"Beast. Look, you come and stay with us. We have a spare room. It's a bit full, but that won't matter."

"Full of what?" he said, curiously.

"Oh, furniture. Oh, you thought people, did you? Heaving bodies. No, no. Our finest antique pieces, I meant. Four poster bed. It was the room they used to keep for the Bishop of Crediton when he came."

"Most suitable," he said. "But I'll have to borrow a boathook."

It was, in fact, most suitable for the Air Vice Marshal's purpose that he should spend a night in this neighbourhood, for the business on which he had come was to make enquiries into an irregular signal received on detectors the night before. The signal had been unfixable, unidentified, and had appeared to go nowhere but into the sea, and had faded before it met the surface.

The whole thing was too vague, but the Air Vice Marshal was a dab hand at killing official uneasiness or finding the way to explain it all away. Like saying to a child, 'It's all right, dear, Daddy's gone to Heaven.'

Joss Couch, landlord, did not ask how they had enjoyed the food, but watched them go with a beady eye, and nodded in reply to their good-night smiles.

"Feudal, he is," Rowena said, outside. "There was a

gassy bitch one night who had Dover sole. 'Oh,' she says, 'no peas?' 'Certainly not,' says he, 'that is Dover sole, landed this morning. Peas are not in season until late May.' So she says, 'But you can get frozen peas!' and he says, '*You* can, madam. I won't.'"

"Like Sue's father," she went on as they approached the car. "He rides his parish on a bloody great horse. Really big. You know, with whiskers round his feet?"

"A shire horse?"

"Right! Knights of old used them because nothing else could carry the weight of armour. Well, her Daddy stands this thing – rather, reverses it, on to the cabbage plot and then prays to the good lord to make it perform. When he doesn't, parson bawls out, 'Shit, for God's sake!' and whirls a football rattle under the horse's ear. Well, of course, the horse's bowels burst asunder with that row."

They stopped at the car.

"I'm just talking because I'm nervous. I like you," she said.

"Don't be nervous. I'm enjoying every minute. The only trouble with that is I want to enjoy too many more."

"You are a sweetie," she said, and kissed him. "Do you know what I think that is up there, over the tower? I think its a fairy snoozing on a bit of cloud he won't let go. He's tied it to his foot."

"How I wish that you were right," he thought and then said, "Well, fairies are not always good, but if he's got a sense of humour he must be. Tied to his foot! What a touch!"

"What are you? I mean, rank?"

"I'm an Air Vice Marshal."

"I'm glad you've got some vice," she said, and got in the car.

He looked up at the sky before he got in. The sky was clear, silver from the almost full moon and inexplicably the ring of light still stayed there.

Or was it a ring? It might be just a blob. A Yank doughnut or a true blue one?

He got into the car. As far as he was concerned, the halo it was a flat tyre. So damned flat one couldn't really see the hole in the middle.

They went to the vicarage. The officer was welcomed. The idea that he should park in the Bishop's bedroom was pronounced very good. He might buy something of the arty objects crowding the room.

But the strange lady of the plasticine was still holding the stage and excited imaginations. The Air Vice Marshal was very interested. He examined it with care, and compared it with Elfrida's books. It seemed he could read Spanish.

"And there was no modelling stuff in the nursery before this morning?" he said. "So it was made between nine and about eighteen hours today. It was found when the boy was asleep. How long do you think he would have been asleep?"

"Well," Susan thought a moment, "supper and bath started about half five, and Leo came back an hour later, or a bit more."

"Quarter to seven," said Arthur. "He could have been asleep half an hour."

"All I wanted to know was whether he could have seen the model," the officer said. "He might not have done. It could have been put on the bed after he went to sleep."

"That would explain why he never said anything," said Leo. "He hadn't got a secret to keep!"

"Where's the rest of this clay stuff?" asked the officer. "Have you actually compared it? Seen how much is missing?"

"Oh," Susan said, "it's the stuff and the amount's about right."

"I got five pounds of it," said Leo. "And most of it's in this."

"I begin to see," said Elfrida. "The boy always has a teddy bear on his pillow?"

"Always," said Sue. "It's his confidant."

"Suppose somebody got in up there," said Elfrida, careless of casting shivers, "knocked this up, then saw the teddy, which is of a shape and changed them over."

"Of a shape?" said Rowena staring. "I never saw a teddy look like that!"

"Form," said Elfrida firmly. "Head then arms, legs, two of each."

"That isn't the pair that catches the eye," said Rowena. "This looks like those idols of women; all tits, bums and belly-buttons, if you pardon the wording, but that's what they look like. I think everybody's right that this is way out even from those."

"We could be being pushed a bit by these photos in the books," said Leo.

The officer went out into the hall and looked around.

"What a lovely place," he said. "The hall, that staircase – you could hire it out for film sets."

He looked up to the top of the stairs with a faraway expression as if he could see up through the walls, the roof and out through the moonlight to the void beyond.

"I have the feeling I was here before," he said. "Perhaps I dreamed I was here . . ."

Three

1

From the moment when Elfrida insisted that she would shack the night on a sofa, it was clear that she was forcing her usual designs on the Air Marshal. It was clearer before midnight that no forcing was necessary.

Leo went upstairs to chisel the lock free on the connecting door off the landing. The door was then stuck open with a wedge underneath it. The flat ceased to be separate.

At one fifteen, the officer and Elfrida were sitting on the edge of the four-poster bed in the moonlight, considering the sexual fantasies of the Incas, which, at first, seemed to have some possible link to the mystery woman of clay, but were proving to have more urgently close complications for Elfrida. The officer was of calmer, deeper appreciation.

The discussion was then as to whether the Incas would have achieved the same satisfaction in a somewhat different way.

Considering her bare breasts with his hands he was undecided.

"I must confess that the matter of the sexual excesses of the Incas is of the utmost imbuggerance to me," said the officer, and persuaded her back on to the bed again.

Suddenly silence fell, and they became still.

"There is someone moving about outside," the officer said.

He got up, snatched a gown, tied it round him by the belt, danced into a pair of slippers and went out into the passage. Elfrida did much the same, and followed him along to the top of the stairs, where he stopped and put a warning hand back to her.

The whole place was quiet and the only lights were from the moon filtering down through the glass ceiling of the hall, and a bright path of moonlight below laid through the kitchen and its open door reaching the side of the staircase wall.

One edge of a shadow was moving, spoiling the straight moonlight line on the hall floor.

"Someone in the kitchen," Elfrida whispered in the officer's ear.

He did not move but stayed staring down at the kitchen doorway. He held up a finger for silence.

There was a soft click, then a broad yellow light crossed the moon path inside the kitchen. Someone had opened the fridge.

A small, childish whisper came up to them as they watched.

"Do you like jelly?"

There was no answer, but after a few seconds there was a tinkle, and then more tinkles and the fridge was shut and the light went off.

"My God! He's feeding it!" hissed Elfrida.

"Might be his teddy bear," said the officer. "Hang on."

The shadow of the boy became clear, elongated on the floor, but there was no other shape on the moon path.

Gawain then came into view and the watchers could see that he had no toy bear with him.

A door opened up on the landing. Elfrida looked back sharply and saw Susan coming out. Elfrida ran back to her, holding up a finger, and somehow she kept the frightened mother quiet a little longer, so she stayed still in the doorway, with Leo close behind her. All three could see down to the moon path from the kitchen door.

The officer stood on the stairs, quite relaxed, hands in his gown pockets, watching the little boy in the kitchen.

Most children have imaginary friends, but they don't normally get up in the middle of the night to feed them. It was this knowledge which held the three on the landing tense and still.

"How do you know there's something there?" Leo whispered.

Elfrida shrugged and signalled for silence again. Susan could hold back no longer. She pushed by. Elfrida grabbed her belt and was left with it hanging in her hand. With the gown flying open like a ghost cloak Susan ran down the stairs to the officer. He raised a hand. She stopped and turned her head to look down at the kitchen again, holding her breath in tight agony.

"Is there somebody with him?" she whispered, letting breath go at last. It made too much noise and the officer grabbed her hand.

At the same moment Rowena appeared through the flat entrance.

"What's the kerfuffle?" she said in a stage hiss. "Burglars? My God! All our stuff—!"

In the kitchen Gawain let out a noise like a leaking boiler.

"Hide, hide, hide! Please hide!"

He seemed to be trying to push something towards the window, but the watchers saw nothing until a faint outline, like a finger shape draw on a water screen, appeared and washed out again almost at once.

"There is something!" Susan cried out and pushed past the officer.

Leo came charging down the stairs. The officer backed away to leave him plenty of room.

"After the bugger!" Leo shouted.

Arthur appeared at the flat entrance, doing up his dressing-gown.

"Burglars!" bellowed Rowena.

"Hold him! I'm coming!" bawled Arthur and charged down the stairs, brandishing a shining Wilkinson piece of sword-work with regimental tassels whirling from the hilt.

Rowena ran down to the officer.

"There's no chance of catching him," he said. "The window is open down there."

Susan swept up the boy and almost smothered him in her palpitating bosom. The boy bawled like a whistle.

"That's my friend! You frightened my friend!" And he cried piercingly.

"Was it a burglar?" said Rowena, holding the officer's arm.

"No. It was a little invisible green man from Capurnia who landed in a saucer and wanted to play with the boy for money. Poker."

She looked at him, then squeezed his arm and started to laugh. Elfrida went by, craning her neck over the rails as if trying to see right through the kitchen window and out in to the wood.

She reached the hall where Susan was trying to comfort the yelling child.

"Poor lamb!" shouted Elfrida. "Does he have to make that bloody row?"

"He's frightened!"

"He's frightened of you. Not his friend. Scaring the man off like that! It might have been the catch of the century, getting in touch with the invisible man from Saturnalia-on-the-Black Hole. Hark at 'em now! Anybody would think they're chasing a wild boar through the wood out there! Silly sods."

She went to the front door, opened it and walked out into the silver moonlight. She listened but heard only the thump and brush of the hunters scratching themselves into rashes on the blackberry bushes.

"The smoke ring's gone," she called back. "Perhaps he landed from it!" She laughed and went out towards the wood which stretched from the side of the house.

The child was snivelling. Susan took him into the kitchen and gave him some milk with half an aspirin in it, although, aided by the rapid recovery of childhood, he was already asleep in her arms when she went to make him drink it.

She started carrying him upstairs. Elfrida came to the open doorway.

"The men are going to keep watch out there for a bit," she said. "Armed guard. Leo did suggest calling the police but it was decided that calling the cops to look for an invisible gargoyle, or whatever it is, wouldn't be that popular. You can't sell stuff like that to coppers, although tracker dogs might swallow it."

"I'm going to sleep in the nursery, anyway," Susan said "Just for a while, I think."

Elfrida went out again. It was such a beautiful night. She came back, listened to make sure nobody was still wandering about in the house, then went back up to the officer's bedroom.

But the four-poster was occupied by more than one. As she stopped at the door she discerned gentle movements and Rowena giggling with pleasure while the air officer chuckled and whispered.

"Blimey!" said Elfrida softly. "*Quel homme*!"

She went downstairs to the sofa.

2

She put on the reading light by the sofa after deciding to keep alert, then got her books, put the little model on the coffee table by her, and with the Spanish dictionary in one hand and the open books laid, one on another, on her knees, she began to work.

Quiet descended.

In about an hour the defenders came back into the hall.

"Hallo," said Leo, looking in at the light. "Are you all right, Elfrida sweetie?"

"Fine."

"Want anything?"

"I've been well satisfied, thanks." She did not look up at all but kept repeating in her head the word she wanted to remember to look for in the dictionary.

"Sure?" said Leo, coming in.

Elfrida lifted her head.

"No. Just shout like hell for Rowena, there's a dear. Quick now. From the hall. Bawl, brother." He went out. She could see Arthur breaking bread in the kitchen for a good-night snack and was relieved.

Leo shouted. He knew what would wake Rowena.

"You be 'right there?" Arthur said, coming in with his mouth full. "You know he wasn't out there. Never got a sight of him. What do you want Ro for?"

"I can't translate this bit." She pointed.

"She doesn't know Spanish!"

"Oh, I thought she did."

Shortly, Rowena came rushing in, bright eyed, smiling.

"Oh, you're back, Arthur!" she said. "What did you want, Elfrida, dear?"

"Safety in numbers," said Elfrida. "I think that's what it says."

Leo looked at her bent over the book. He was suspicious, but he said nothing.

"Where's the visiting officer?" said Arthur.

"In bed," said Elfrida. "He realised it was no good. Leave me to wrestle with this."

They went upstairs. Elfrida called up suddenly.

"Oh, Susan's sleeping in the nursery, Leo!"

"Okay. I won't disturb. Might wake Gaw."

Quiet came again. She wrestled on. The picture began to build up in her mind of a long-ago invasion, but having no real grasp of the language under the spotting-word system the mental picture was built on very long legs from the basic original guesswork. It was becoming enthralling.

At one time she looked up and realised that the church clock had not rung for some hours. She shrugged and went back to the book.

There seemed to be no doubt in the book that some kind of invasion by aliens had taken place between four and seven thousand years ago. It might have been a full-scale affair, with landings all over the globe, or probably a series of landing parties, raiders looking for loot.

What loot was here that might not be elsewhere? If there were something here which wasn't elsewhere, how could it be valuable to them? Raiders loot things that will make them rich, and a merchant won't get rich selling something the buyer doesn't recognise as anything at all.

The original theory was that it was a research landing and the astronauts had never seen women before and so had much to learn.

She chuckled quietly.

But most speculation on such invasions is based on the idea that the invaders' world is dying and they need somewhere new to live. *Lebensraum.*

But supposing they were dying from lack of *women*?

Supposing they had raided, found the world with women in a great majority and saw the opportunity to export thousands back to their own place and stock up?

Elfrida was surprised at her idea, and even began to wonder how she had thought of such a thing. Perhaps it was perverseness; opposing the existing idea.

The statuette had been made by alien means from alien clay, and left, perhaps accidentally. Right. That ruled out the idea that the invaders might have been women, for they would have a better idea of what they looked like than this exaggeration.

No, she began to think her idea right. The world had been populated mainly by women at that time. The women were the loot. The original model perhaps having been made by some lecturer riding in a spaceship bringing the raiders to earth.

For such a purpose the figure would have been excellent, showing the umistakable differences between the human sexes.

"I am becoming women dominated," she said, and shook her head as if to clear it. "But woman is the constant. In nature, she is supreme, the male a means to an end. But, oh my, what a lovely end to the means, now I come to recall."

She often spoke to herself, like Susan. Now she stopped and looked towards the window. No one had pulled the curtains. She could see the church tower, serene against the silver night. It was clear, and the fish-skin of the slates on the roof-slope butting the tower, shone under the moon.

She turned off the reading lamp. The church tower and the west end of the roof were magnificent, with no shading of the moonlight.

"I think," she said, patting her knee as if in self-encouragement, "I think something's here. Oh Christ!" she added very quietly.

By some instinct she knew it was not outside the window, but somewhere inside the room.

Inside her head she addressed a great hall of shadows, saying, "There must be beings somewhere in the universe who do not reflect our light and therefore may be invisible to us here but are seen at home, where we, if we went with them across space, might be invisible in our turn. Thus, no one should be afraid of what is a natural phenomenon. And I may say, in ancient cant, all that is a lot of rubbish and I am about to pee myself with fright."

She even heard her own voice echoing in the phantom hall inside her head, and her whole body went skin tight with fear.

Deliberately, she put the books carefully on the seat beside her and then got up. There was no sound in the room. She turned and went into the hall, walking slowly, firmly, and near the door the moon shone on the upper blade and hilt of the Wilkinson sword Arthur had parked in an elephant's-foot umbrella stand.

She went to it, hesitated and looked up the stairs. It was quiet everywhere. The front door was still wide open as she had left it and the others had used it.

She put her fingers on the sword hilt, then changed her mind, turned and went back into the room. She halted for a second, then deliberately walked to the window.

The tension in her suddenly eased. Nothing was there.

A feeling of excitement filled her; a sensation of assurance, of command. She walked back to the sofa, turned and went to the window. She untied her sash and opened the gown, put her fists on her bare thighs and looked to where she had known something had been watching her, but nothing was there. She laughed.

"Hell! It's just a ghost. Something the child invented. Something we all took for granted because of one, lonely little boy.

We are all frightened by one little boy who had a message from the heavens and faked up a plastic woman because he couldn't help it. Nobody was here. Nobody could have been here. Nobody, nobody at all. It might have been done with a spoon-handle because he was receiving the message and had to do as he was told. A biblical story, repeated oft—.

She went into the hall and up the stairs and turned by the nursery door to go to the Bishop's bedroom. She stopped for a moment to hear heavy snoring coming from inside the room, then went on.

The Bishop's door was partly open. She stopped again as she heard a girl laugh softly in the room. Curious, even wondering, she looked in at the moonlit scene. The officer was sitting on a stool and Susan, her beltless gown wide open, was sitting astride the officer.

She was laughing because he was making small, amusing noises with his lips on her breasts.

"My God! He's at it again!" breathed Elfrida, backing away. "That's not a *homme*, that's Ingredient X."

She went downstairs and out into the moonlight, surprised, excited again. She could understand the officer. There was something very odd in the air that night, a weird exhilaration. It was more than the effect of a warm night or full moon, but something familiar, yet entirely strange; something that should always have been there and never had been, quite.

"The moon dance," said Elfrida, dropping off her gown and kicking off her sandals. "A tribute to Spring and Pan and the nymphs laughing as they fly, trailing translucent gossamer through the woods."

She began to dance in a way that vaguely imitated a native moon dance she had seen in Sumatra, a quiet place, the back of nowhere, of private rituals and the rare scent of roasting pork lingering in the great trees of the forest like spirits trailing up through the leaves.

She had moved over the lawn close to the edge of the wood when she felt a curious warm and sensuous brush all over the front of her body. For a moment she kept dancing slowly but then realised it felt like being embraced by some curious movement of silky warm air.

She stopped still, her eyes moving quickly and seeing nothing near her at all. The touch was still there on her body, so light she began to think it must be nothing more than an unusual rising current of air.

Then another memory startled her. Once, sleeping

on a veranda during a night of jungle heat, she had been wakened by what she had thought was someone touching her gently. She had opened her eyes to see a snake moving over her bare body, exploring. She had known then that if she moved, she would most likely be soon dead in great pain, so she stayed still. The movement and touch of the snake had been the opposite to anything she had ever imagined in nightmares. It was cool, silky, dry, erotic. When it slid off her to the floor and moved away under the bottom of the net she had sat up and nearly fainted.

The sensation she felt by the wood was like the snake somehow; the same sinuous silky movement on her skin.

She jumped backwards, then ran a few paces towards the house, stopped and looked back. There was nothing in front of the trees; nothing to be seen, but there had been something there all right.

She bent down and squatted on her heels, looking along the grass towards the wood, as if a shadow might show in the movement of the grass as someone trod on it. She saw nothing of a movement.

She thought again of her ideas that seven thousand years ago the raiders had come for women to take back.

The raiders who had left their statuette.

The statuette exactly the same as the plastic model made up in the playroom:

She stood up, shuffled into her sandals, then bent and picked up the borrowed gown. She stood there holding it, still looking towards the wood. Then she turned her head slowly and looked up to the sky above the church tower.

The light ring had not come back. The clock had not struck.

Her mind darted about.

Invaders were now invisible? Seven thousand years is a long time for science. A lot of things can be found out.

And one thing that might be found out is how to send messages to simple humans without any invader being there. Signals persuading them, rousing them, pleasing them,

"After all," said Elfrida aloud, "if I get pleased, I warm up and give way. Doesn't everybody?"

She slipped the gown over her shoulders and went across the grass and into the wood. The moonlight and young leaves left a dappled pattern on the ground as she walked through until she came out on the rising ground beyond.

In the quiet of the night she could hear the sea murmuring beyond the headland. She turned and looked across the silver waters of the estuary.

"Something's here," she said. "But how can the child see him when we can't? He offered it jelly!"

In all the excitement of chasing the burglar, no one had looked at the jelly. No one had mentioned it.

She went back into the house and the kitchen. There was a chair in the gap beside the fridge and the dresser. The glass jelly bowl was on the seat, as if the boy had put it there. She picked it up and carried it to the open window. She did not switch on the light. She was in spiritual commune with the moonglow and sudden change of light might break her thoughts.

The jelly had mostly gone, scraped out by what looked like a large grooved spoon.

"Oh God," she said. "A claw?"

She felt the soft, silky touch on her breast again, as if coaxing her to leave the bowl and submit and say nothing.

She backed away from the window and stopped. She put the bowl on the table and stayed looking out to the wood.

"Not claws," she said, and turned away. "I'm imagining. I must be. It's a trick. A feelie. We were going to have feelie films once, but they thought they'd better not." She laughed, and turned and went back to the window, and stood there, gown hanging open from her shoulders. "Well, come on then. The more we experience, the more we get to know."

She felt the touch smooth across her belly and she pulled the muscles in sharply, as if suddenly walking waist-deep in water. She relaxed after a few seconds.

The touch stopped when she had recoiled, like an understanding lover, and when she eased, it began again, smoothing, moulding.

She let it go on and then put her hands out slowly, but her fingers touched nothing.

"You must be there," she said. "Tell me about yourself. Please tell me who you are."

She drew her hands back and let them fall to her sides. She closed her eyes and let the sensations of pleasure flow through her.

"Tell me. Just tell me who you are," she whispered.

And suddenly she was taken. She seemed like a bird flying along close on top of a field of dandelion puffs, but the field was blue and black and green and purple and all colours, creating an immense depth beyond the range of an eye, and the puffballs were stars; stars brightening and dying, turning and falling, trailing specks of light down into an abyss which swallowed nothing. There was no sensation of speed, or flying, or of anything but the soft embrace which held her entirely, so that fear no longer existed.

She was approaching a star which swelled bigger and bigger in the deep void in front of her until she thought it must burst, but the brilliance of it faded and a place of great vertical lines grew round her, a huge place; a cathedral. She could still see the faint gleaming of the stars through the vertical flutes of the walls and columns which formed this place, as if it were all made of black glass.

There were transparent blocks around her, oblongs, standing upright, dull, deep multi-coloured glass.

She became aware of some sort of transmissions coming to her first from one, then another, like people talking but making no sound that she could hear. Her brain began to buzz, and for an instant she stiffened and began to resist, but then the soft, deep caress began to soothe her again and she felt at peace, happy, with no fear of these things.

Something seemed to be flicking in her head, but it did not matter. It was some game they were playing, asking her something, sending their messages direct into her brain, because the blocks had no mouths. It was all very simple. A child could understand it. A child was understanding it.

Abruptly the whole scene was withdrawn as if she

had suddenly retreated from the cathedral and the planet it stood on so fast that it was like watching a balloon go down. She shut her eyes. The rate of retreat was so fast it pulled her brain out in trying to understand what was happening.

The soft, assuring caress was no longer there on her skin and she felt real fear take command of her whole being. But there was hard ground under her knees. She was not falling or moving anywhere.

Dazed she opened her eyes and looked at the wet dewy grass sparkling in the morning sun. She felt too stunned to realise that she had come back. She kept her head down, looking at the grass, and then she began to laugh and all the pressure of hysteria drifted away on the warm air.

Four

1

Breakfast was in progress. Arthur was taking his standing up, *The Times* in one hand, a coffee cup in the other. Leo scowled at some letters that had just come in the post. He did not like bills. He had a pathological hatred of bills.

"I'm broke," he said. "The hell with it!"

"More toast?" asked Rowena at the cooker and smiled happily at him.

"God knows what you have to be so cheerful about in the morning," Leo said. "I don't remember too much of it, personally."

"It's a new day," said Rowena.

"Where's that bloody woman?" said Arthur.

"What, Susan?" said Leo.

"No, Elfrida. I suppose she wants a lift back, doesn't she? I'm here, waiting about; appointments coming up and the whole parade of Flapdoodle in preparation for a suckers' carnival."

"You go," said Rowena. "I'll lift her."

"Okay. Explain. Apologise." He left the coffee cup, took *The Times* and went.

Leo asked, "Aren't you coming in, then?"

"Not till later," Rowena said, making toast. "You've got Mrs. Bifocals and her punchy daughter to run things."

Leo got up. "Where's the Air Marshal or whatever he is?"

"On the phone. Very important. He's been half an hour already. Don't anybody worry. It's all Government reverse-charge stuff. You can't lose."

"Very amusing chap," said Leo.

"Quite fun," said Rowena, picking out toast.

The officer came in.

"I have an awful request to make," he said, smiling and looking from one to the other. "May I hang on to the Bishop's room for one more night? I could go down to the pub, but I enjoyed myself so much, with the informality and interesting chat. It's so far away from our world of aircraft, missiles and electronic ironmongery, and something has cropped up which I've got to look into hereabouts."

"Say no more," said Leo.

"Of course," said Rowena, buttering hot toast. "Nobody's using the room, if you don't mind the jumble up there."

"I love jumble," said the officer. "And it is very lovely jumble, isn't it? It must be worth a mint."

Susan came in behind him. "Gawain's gone to play in the woods. He's going to collect primroses." She turned and smiled at the officer. "Did you make your call?"

"I hope I wasn't obstructing the line," he said. "But I would like to make another call, if I may? And leave your number?"

"Help yourself," said Leo.

"Thanks." The officer went out to the small room known as the office.

"You girls look very pleased with yourselves this morning," said Leo, cocking his head.

"Well, it's a fine day," said Susan and kissed him. "Something in the air, you know? Even Gaw's got nature, going out to dig in the woods."

"I hope he finds truffles," Leo said.

"You don't like truffles," Rowena said.

"No. But I can sell 'em." He looked at his watch. "It's funny about Elfrida. You say she left her clothes?"

"Well, *you* know what she is about clothes," said Susan. "She's probably out doing a dew dance or something."

The officer came back. "Fixed," he said. "And many thanks. I am grateful. Perhaps I may take you all to dinner tonight? We can go early and bring Gawain, then no sitter's wanted. If we could fix it now, I have to be out all day."

"Of course," Leo said.

"If I may beg a little more," the officer said, "would you drop me off at a car rental place? I must have one and service vehicles come complete with driver. I prefer the Lone Ranger aspect."

They went.

"Did he have any breakfast?" said Rowena.

"I don't know," Susan said. "I haven't."

Twenty minutes later, Elfrida came in, still in the borrowed gown.

"Where have you been?" Rowena said. "You look

as if you've been dragged through a hedge backwards."

"I think I've been rather prettily raped," Elfrida said.

"I should have thought that impossible," said Susan, with a tight, small smile.

"I have been raped twice before," said Elfrida, pouring out tea. "Once in Burma when I never saw a thing but felt a lot, and in a disco in Peru where the boy wasn't quite sure what he was doing, but as he had a knife I thought I'd better let him. I was married, so I was used to it."

"Well, all right," said Rowena, impatiently. "But what happened this time?"

Elfrida told.

Rowena wriggled. "Erg," she said. "I don't think I want to be touched up like that!"

"I thought if I let myself go I might learn what's going on."

"I'd better see that Gaw's all right," said Susan, turning from washing-up to grab a towel.

"He's all right, Susan," the woman said. "It's friendly. The little boy knows it. After all, if he wasn't, would Gawain have been safe up till now?"

"She's right, Sue," Rowena said. "Don't mumfuss. Now. You went and you saw stars – no, I don't mean that funny – and these blocks flicking things into your head. Do you mean you flicked back?"

"I don't know," Elfrida sat back, leaning her arms over the back of the chair. "I keep trying to find connections."

"We know that," said Susan.

"Between one thing and another," the woman added, "there is spring in the air. Randy is rampant. All right. It always is one way or another. But last night. We all know what happened with the Air Vice Marshal. How old would you say he is?"

"A magnificent forty," said Rowena.

"He must be more," said Susan thoughtfully, and then concentrated. "Where are we going, anyway?"

"It was a point I wondered about," Elfrida said. "Because he is very high brass indeed, I think he must be fifty."

"Well, I don't much care," Rowena said. "It doesn't affect everybody the same."

"Anyhow, to start with, I thought he was charming and intelligent and obviously very much interested in that doll," said Elfrida. "Right? Then about half past eleven, when we'd all broken up for bed, I felt the most impulsive urge for him and I went upstairs and he knew. And he was somehow different. Much younger, older, no age at all. Age didn't come into it. It was just something I wanted to do or burst. You understand me? I was flirting a bit before, perhaps, but purely for amusement."

She shrugged.

"Do you know, you didn't get mixed up once, saying all that?" said Susan.

The woman leaned forward and drank some tea.

"Tell me, did he suggest anything to you before you went in there?" she said, and looked from one to the other.

Rowena started to laugh a little helplessly. "Well, I – I don't know. Yes, I think I do. I felt like you, I just wanted to. He must have some tremendous magnetism."

"He's got more than that," said Susan, staring out of the window. "He was so inventive. As if I was the only partner he'd ever studied, and study is the word. I don't think I ever remember anything like it. The detail—" She shook her head and then shrugged as if she couldn't think of words to fit.

"And would you do it again?" said Elfrida, watching.

Rowena pulled a face. "I don't think I could help it. It was so delightfully naughty, improper. Yes. Wouldn't you?"

"The point is made," said Elfrida. "He had something at night which wasn't there during the evening. He was normally attractive and charming, and then suddenly a tremendous aura, a feeling of indispensable – no; a sort of imperative something you always wanted to do but always stood back a bit and suddenly it all didn't matter and it was glorious and we knew it would be before we went in there."

Susan looked out of the windowstill. Rowena fiddled with breadcrumbs.

"Why analyse it?" said Susan.

"I was not analysing him but the aura," said the woman. "The aphrodisiac transmission from the Bishop's room, pulling us one after the other, not altogether; not one turning up at the wrong time, as if we had all agreed—"

"Oh, it's silly to go on like that!" said Susan, shortly.

"And ungrateful," said Rowena.

"What *are* you trying to get at, Elfrida?" said Susan.

"The splendour of fertility rites in the Bishop's room, and the deliberate attack on my moral armour by the sensations which finally got me going to where the hell I did go. Pan."

"Pan!" said Rowena. "Well, we all know he hasn't got a goat's back end."

"Look, Elfrida, I agree that it was unusual, but it happened and I don't see why we should hold a court of enquiry into it. You've got yourself wound up with the doll, the spacemen, the church, black magic, smoke rings and being touched by somebody who wasn't there, who took you for a ride and ran out of petrol at the old convenient moment. And if you're almost right, and it's magic of some sort, well—"

"Let's have some more," said Rowena and laughed.

Elfrida stood up. "I thought I'd point it out. That's all. It might come in useful. I'd better dress."

"You'll be able to test your theory, dear," said Susan, smiling. "He's staying another night, and you're welcome to make a scientific study."

"Staying again, is he? I wonder if it will happen twice?"

"Easily," said Rowena.

The front door bell started ringing. Elfrida took her clothes up to the bathroom. Once in there she started to run a bath and looked at herself in the mirror.

"They know something's wrong, and they like it. But what is happening? Are the visitors really going to land again, after all this time? Or have they already?"

She got into the bath. Someone knocked at the door.

"It's me. Susan. I've brought you some towels."

"Come right in. Your lock's busted, anyway."

"Oh, I keep meaning to tell Leo," Susan said, coming in with an armful of towels. "I'll shove them on the chair. Can you reach?"

The door fell to. Susan sat on the pile of towels.

"Do you really mean that what you said about this, sort of touching you?"

Elfrida sat up. "Have you had it?"

"No."

"You mean, am I imagining? Certainly not. I have tested quite a few witch doctors and conjurors. I am an enquirer."

"Yes, yes. I know." Susan looked at the wall. "You've made me feel odd, but I think I should have felt odd before. It's the first time I ever went in to my husband - either one, of course - and said, 'You take over in the nursery. I need a rest.' I did it last night. And I was so tight and excited because I was doing it that I didn't bother to think outside what I wanted to do. I didn't bother about the deception, the unfaithful—"

She made fists and hit them together twice and then laughed.

"That sounds absurd, but the four of us have been all together for such a long time. Then we paired off and married. Then somebody said about the wife-swop and so we did, and after that we swopped when we felt like it. But it's never seemed unfaithful because all four always stayed together, knew each other, knew what everybody felt and what they did.

"But last night I deliberately got Leo into the nursery to snore on there while I went in for a love session with a man I hadn't known for a day."

"Do you always wait longer than a day?" Elfrida said, soaping her arms. "I've always found if I wait to think I don't."

"Now you're just getting sexy and deliberately shifting away from what we were talking about!" Susan was angry.

"I'm not. I'm investigating bit by bit. But get back to the start. Is it all unusual? Yes. It is unusual. Has it happened before? No, it hasn't happened before. Has anything that happened yesterday happened before? No, not in the way it did then. Is that what you mean?"

"Yes."

"And that's what I mean, too. Would you bury the hatchet and scrub my back?"

"Of course. Give me the loofah. It's stuck under your toes." Elfrida bent, and handed up the loofah, staying bent to expose her back. "The trouble is, we have something here and I think we all ought to know about it, but we can't tell the men, now, can we?"

Elfrida chuckled at the water. "No. You can't. It would be cumbersome, to coin a phrase."

Susan went to scrub her back then stopped.

"You've got funny marks on your back. Did you know?"

"What sort of funny marks?" Elfrida put a hand back to feel.

"Hold still. It looks like muddy smears, but it hasn't come off in the water. Did you rub across something? A bush, or—"

"Is it scratched?"

"No. Keep still. It looks like streaks of dye. Perhaps

you got it from grass. It's greenish. Never mind. What are we going to tell them?"

"You can't tell them anything about last night, not like that," said Elfrida. "Are you taking my skin off?"

Susan straightened up. "They won't come off. The marks."

"Give me that hand-mirror," Elfrida said. "No, you have it. I'd better get out. I can never work out exactly how to hold the mirrors to see my back." She got out and stood in front of the long mirror on the wall. Susan held the hand-glass.

"You see?" Susan said.

"It looks as if I was hotly cuddled by a printer with inky paws—" Elfrida stopped and looked down. "My God, its not anywhere else, is it?"

Susan just stared at the marks. "You don't mean it might be *him*? Hell!" She undid her checked shirt and pulled it off over her head, then unzipped her slacks, let them fall and stood naked, looking anxiously into the mirror. "Have I?" she said anxiously, turning her back. "Have I got any?"

"No." Elfrida smacked her bottom. "You're not marked for export."

"What do you mean?" Susan said, turning to her.

"Oh, I didn't tell— Never mind! You haven't got any marks! I tell you. Don't panic!"

"What do you mean, marked for export? Is there something you know you haven't told?"

Rowena bawled from outside. "Where are you, Sue? For God's sake, I've looked everywhere!"

The bathroom door pushed open. Rowena looked in.

"What are you doing?" she said, blankly. "There's somebody—"

"Elfrida's got marks," Susan said. "Look! They won't wash off!"

Rowena came in. "There's a couple complaining downstairs. Heavens! You must have been cuddling the tar man. About last—"

"They came last night," said Susan. "Those marks."

"Why won't they wash off?" Elfrida asked. "Surely it couldn't have been him? A joke? He wouldn't have done it, would he? That would be a bit unfunny!"

"Him?" said Rowena, staring at the woman's back. "Oh golly, no! He wouldn't, would he? Susan, zip me. I just want to be sure. Arthur wasn't very - I don't know, just a bit off this morning."

Susan zipped the dress. "You're all right, far as I can see. It must have been something Elfrida— Good God!" She put a hand to her mouth and stared at the woman's back. "They're fading! Fading away!"

Elfrida put a hand round to feel her back. "But I'm dry now, aren't I? Almost. Wipe it with a towel. Quick!"

Susan swept up a towel and rubbed across the marks, one way then the other. She looked at the towel. It was unstained.

Elfrida turned. "Nothing there?"

"Perhaps it was a heat blush, from the water, you know," said Rowena. "These downstairs people are going to burst— Ooo!"

Susan looked at her. Elfrida looked at Susan. Seeing

two pairs of eyes looking at her chest, Susan looked down.

Two green circles were shining on her breasts like a pair of comic spectacles.

"It's light!" said Elfrida. "It's got to be light. It's a trick. Humorous again. Trying to be friendly."

"There's something in here!" Susan said looking round the ceiling wildly. "Outside! Quick!"

The woman grabbed up her clothes but was last out, looking keenly all round as if hoping to see it somewhere amongst the steam from the bath. Then she began to laugh and went out to the others.

They went into Susan's bedroom.

"It's trying to make contact all the time, you see?" Elfrida said. "That's the point. Gawain can respond, but perhaps we're too hidebound."

Susan was looking anxiously in the mirror, then whistled with relief. "They've gone," she said. "Phew! I nearly jumped through the bloody ceiling. Friendly? I don't want any more of that kind."

"The interesting part is that the marks followed me about in there," said Elfrida. "You know, in the bath and when I got out, so it's got to be just in the bathroom."

"Oh my God! These people!" gasped Rowena, turning to the door. "You've got to come, Sue. It's a protest committee."

"Protest about what?"

"Us," said Rowena. "I can't face it alone. I'll go and keep them quiet."

"Give them Leo's cigars," said Susan struggling into slacks.

"One's a woman," said Rowena. "You hurry." She went out.

"It's a trick with light," said Elfrida in another world.

"It's all sorts of tricks," said Susan shortly. "What about feeling you all over? Is that light?"

"Frequency. I've read you get tingles from certain frequencies, and if you have a lot of it you could get the sensation of being touched."

"What we need is an exorcist."

"This is nothing to do with the devil. It's a visitation from upwards, not downwards."

"Anyhow," Elfrida went on, "there must have been a reason for painting us like that. Do you know what I think? It was an experiment in pigmentation. These people are invisible here, but they probably know we're scared off from anything like that and they're experimenting with ways of making themselves seen. What sort of light reflects on flesh?"

"It must have been instructive for them to see what I look like as a pair of pop-eyed sunglasses," said Susan and suddenly laughed, but reduced it to a grin to paint her lips at the mirror.

Elfrida dressed by the bed.

"It was real horror," Susan went on, buttoning a shirt. "Thinking of something in there with us that I couldn't see, nobody could see. I was all goose-pimples and then – I don't know whether it's being out of the bathroom, but it seems funny. Something trying to make us laugh. Just as you said. Like a little boy trying hard. You know what I mean? Impish. That's what it seems like now. Perhaps it's reaction, relief. Whatever.

Well, I'll have to see this Grump brigade. Come if you like. Moral support. It can't be private if it's a protest. I hope they haven't brought banners. Half the buggers can't spell. I once saw a union banner saying, 'We won't be treated like surfs'. Non-U at its worst."

2

I was interested to observe the reaction of these ladies to what was no more than a humorous experiment with light. It produced surprising exhibitions of something which I didn't hear much of before, in 17 – whatever year it was then. It is something they call guilt, which appears to mean simply a fear of being found out. This quality has even attained the status of having a *complex*, but, then, I have noticed before that man's main occupation is to complicate almost everything he can lay his mind to.

Here we have these people alarmed by the thought of something they can't see. They reduce everything to something they can see; that is, there had to be *something* in the bathroom to paint them green. Once they imagine there is some *thing*, they seem to feel better, and yet, when they have such a thing under their noses, they immediately think it is something else.

The human has a very difficult philosophy to follow, and I think it best summed up by an earth fellow I overheard say: "It can't possibly happen to me. And if it does it can't possibly happen twice. Can it?"

Five

1

The visitors seemed horrifying. The man was tall, thin, in a black suit, white shirt, dark grey tie, held a black felt hat, was thin and hang-jawed, baggy under the eyes, hawk-nosed, bald with grey side tufts pulled out like stub wings, and a mouth like a zip zipped.

Rowena noted.

The woman was large, wide, shiny black high-heeled shoes, brick-red suit buttoned once in the middle so her top almost spilled out wide like a bulldozer front; round Dutch doll face, glass-blue eyes, flaxen, assisted hair and a shining straw up-turned-basin hat off face.

Rowena memorised.

Rowena was alone with them for five minutes until Susan came. In that time she offered coffee, the weather, last year's roses, crime, Government, films and television plays. In return she got: They've taken the rose down. There wasn't a rose in here. It was the next room. It was here. I would have been standing right under it; under the rose, *sub rosa*; they have taken it down. I say it was in the next room, the next room, the next room, and I remember when the Bishop was here he got his crook to reflect in it, the painting was so fresh, and that was in the next room. I distinctly remember it was in this small room, because there is no point in having a rose in a large room. It was in the next room. You wouldn't have taken the rose down, would you? Last year's rose? Oh, ceiling rose. There is one in the small room the other side of the hall.

Frozen silence melted by Susan coming in with Elfrida.

Introductions: Councillor Trelawney, Councillor Watts, mumble, mumble, fruit and bumble, do, do, do, do?

About the church. The people still feel about it as if it were their church and their feelings are of concern to us, as we have to soak them all up and put them into some sort of words to try to invent a discussion, the result of which will assure them their interests have been looked after, which as it's their church and they feel very strongly about it not being their church and the fact they never went to it for twenty-five years is neither here nor there, the church being their heritage, quite apart from God and other considerations and they are concerned with nightmares and fears of devolution, devilry, dissipation and sodomy within the sancturary of esseldom, and while we are aware it is now your church, we are nevertheless required to think of it as not your church but their church and are thus concerned with the unusual stories and rumours of a frightening kind about their church, our church, their church, our church, deeds, deeds, deeds, deeds, and money, ours, ours, ours spiritually, the province of the people, people, people, who never went to it, deserted it, deserted it.

"We are getting nowhere," observed Councillor Watts, mopping his bald brow.

"What is that?" said Councillor Trelawney pointing to the figure on the mantelpiece with a hand jingling with rings and bracelets.

Elfrida, who was seething with indignation and determined not to be steamrollered by the Council tits, said, "That is an ancient Peruvian frotting piece."

"It is disgusting," said Trelawney.

"So were the ancient Peruvians," said Elfrida. "But civilisation is a varied import, foreign to the indigenous in emotional ways, but accepted as a means of keeping what is one's own."

"A Bolshevist?" whispered Trelawney to her companion.

"Really?" said Watts, sweating profusely and dabbing generously. "Frotting, is that some fertility ceremony or some such?"

"Very much fertility," said Elfrida (introduced as world traveller and propagationologist). "Much like the very old Anglican ceremony of flogging the bishop." She looked at the figure critically.

Susan turned away. Rowena just stood beaming at the visitors.

"Low church, one assumes?" said Trelawney.

"Very," said Elfrida. "There is some doubt as to whether the figure is the work of ancient Peru, or of an artist from another planet."

Trelawney said, "Whaaat?"

Watts said, "I should have thought it too earthy. In the summer we have a lot of trouble with graffiti or, as *I* think it should be, rude things on walls."

"Cave men wrote everything on walls," said Elfrida. "Films and television still do."

"I hadn't thought of that," said Watts with grateful interest. "I—"

"William!" said Trelawney, in particular and then in general. "Not to put too fine a point on it, the main concern about the church amongst people is the – well, it is a rumour, but very disturbing for all that, and it is that there is some intention of turning it over to some sort of devil worship, and now I hear you say this – this *thing* is some kind of alien product, which is – both are somewhat of the same, and that, er, what figure is somewhat similar to—"

She broke off and looked down behind her, then from one side to the other across the floor. Then she looked sharply at Councillor Watts but he was edging earnestly towards Elfrida with the idea of learning more, and, she realised, too far forward to have had his hand in any such position.

She looked ahead again, then moved her body slightly and uneasily, from one side to the other and looked behind again.

Susan noticed her movement, and said, "Let's all sit down and discuss this over some sherry. It's early, I know, but this is a tricky little subject for us all and my husband has some very special sherry from I forget where and it is soothing."

"It is very kind," said Trelawney, "and I am getting a little weary of standing up for justice and democracy." She laughed and looked briefly behind her again.

"Meg?" said Watts, in a curious tone.

Meg stood for a moment or two longer as if testing her decision, and then said, "The subject is difficult and I don't think it's going to be successfully examined—" she broke off, paused, rose a little off her heels, looked at the mantelpiece and right through to the other side. "Oh let's sit down!" she said desperately.

Susan went for sherry. Elfrida went on with men from space and he said he had seen this film on television, another in cinema and specially that, because of censorship and it didn't matter, even if it was right in the middle of some big scientific scene a couple might start fucking any moment and it was difficult.

At that point Councillor Watts became still.

"What sort of business are you in?" said Susan, covering pleasantly.

"Er, building," said Watts, puzzled and horrified, both at once. "It is very warm for the season," he added, running a handkerchief round the inside of his collar. For relief he watched Rowena trying to light a cigarette. She was trembling and couldn't get the end in the flame.

"Seriously," said Elfrida - they were all seated in a ring - "what do people think is going on?"

"I beg your pardon?" said Trelawney suddenly, clearly jerked from some other consideration. "Where? Oh! At the church! Yes."

Watts leant sideways and whispered, "You are evading the issue, Meg. This is official business, and we have to report." He leant the other way to Elfrida, "And you think that these landings—?"

Rowena was watching Councillor Trelawney with some interest. The councillor looked as if she wanted to slap somebody and giggle, and while trying to listen to Councillor Watts she started resting her hands on her open neckline of blouse as if to stop anyone getting his hand in there. So Rowena thought.

They drank sherry. Susan poured generously. It was easing things along. Or the general atmosphere was easing things along. Or Elfrida was easing Councillor Watts along. Susan didn't mind which, so long as things eased along.

She was not herself too sure about Arthur's plans for the church. She had never been quite sure of any of Arthur's plans.

"It will be a place of renewed interest for the townspeople," she said, catching Councillor Watts from Elfrida.

Rowena smiled at Councillor Trelawney. "Have you ever heard of this house being haunted?" she said, leaning forward.

"I - er—" she leant closer to Rowena and whispered.

Rowena smiled. Both stood up, excused themselves and went out into the hall, closing the door behind them. Rowena indicated the cloakroom, but the fat lady caught her arm.

"No, I don't want to go, dear. An excuse." She looked around and appeared to be relieved in some way.

"What's the matter?" Rowena said. "I noticed you

were fidgety before I said about haunting."

"Yes. That's a good word. Fidgety." She looked back at the door of the room and put a hand to her behind. "Someone— Let me put this as a proposition. Forget logic, common sense, all that. Someone was feeling my bottom when I was standing up. No! don't say anything. No one was near. I looked. I don't usually look, nor, I suppose, would you. One rejects. In my years in the council chambers one gets used to fumbles. God knows, we've all had to get used to fumbles, but this was, I dare not say *professional* because I wouldn't know, but one imagines what am I talking about."

"I know what you mean," Rowena said. "Elfrida, that's Mrs Elton, told us she had some odd sensations last night."

"My dear girl, this was more than an odd sensation. It was so confident, pleasant, one might even say. Then when I sat down it began up here." She gestured. "I just had to come out." She took Rowena's arm and looked into her face. "What is it?" she whispered.

Rowena shook her head helplessly. "I don't know. We didn't even believe Elfrida when she said. When we talked we thought it might be some kind of air current, off the heating perhaps."

"This was no air current. This was a determined prelude to seduction!" said Trelawney. "And if there'd been *anyone there* I could see I might—" She stopped. "You haven't *got* an invisible man? There are so many idiotic inventions these days." She put fingers to her temples. "Do you believe, I wasn't like this when I came? It isn't your sherry. I am a shy person. People say formidable, and I am because I'm frightened, so I try to look firm. So there I am looking firmly at you and suddenly a soft, lingering hand starts feeling my bum as if he was chuckling intimately in my ear at the same time. You know what I mean?"

"I can't wait so find out!" Rowena laughed and so did the Councillor, then she was serious again. "Honestly, it's nothing we know about. Never heard of it till this morning. Honestly."

"I'm not going to mention it to my husband," Trelawney said, looking round again, abstractedly. "He's a retired colonel. Always laughing at women. He'd grab at this. Jokes about grandiose illusions of menopause. Let's be serious.

"If there is some wandering spirit of lust in there, he'd be pretty stupid to choose me, considering the choice. How did I get it?"

"Were you doing anything at the time? Thinking of something?"

"No. No I was trying desperately to see how this meeting could be of any use because we have nothing but airy rumour to go on and the church is yours, which to me ends the matter. Well, I've ended anyhow. I've lost my bold front. I always have to work up so to get it, and now it's gone, but I can't let my colleague know. I'll have to don armour again. The breastplates of authority— There was one thing. That little idol. It fascinated with its ugliness. I kept looking at it— Well, I feel better now. I always envied anyone living in this house. So beautiful. I'm not going off my nut. I'm fifty-seven and I don't feel things unless I've actually got them. My flesh doesn't imagine and get sensations. I am a very sturdy, thick-headed woman and anything more solid than that I wouldn't know."

She turned and looked at Rowena.

"I just don't know what to say," Rowena said. "I've tried. It doesn't work."

"I must go back. But if I'm going to feel anything more extensive I shall scream. In fact," she said, straightening her straw hat by means of the hall mirror, "it might do me good. Even my husband might say, 'Good God! What's that noise?' If I screamed at breakfast. Once I got used to it, I mean."

They went back into the room.

"Sorry to have gone," said the councillor. "Have you sorted anything out?"

"Oh yes," said Susan, smiling. "Mr. Watts is going to come and put all our locks and things right for us. That's a weight off my mind. It's a week's work."

Councillor Watts smiled at his colleague, then wiped his brow.

The meeting ended with Watts making some notes of what they had said, while Trelawney sat in a state of suspended expectancy, but the lusty ghost seemed to have gone.

"While we're here, might we look inside the church?" Watts asked mildly. "It's just a question of satisfying the committee."

"Of course," Susan said, impatiently. "Mrs. Marchant will show you. I must find my child and see what he's up to. You'll excuse me. It's been so nice and so forth and fluff and verbal spindrift, goodbye."

Rowena and Elfrida took them into the church. It was

a vast echoing emptiness. The pews, pulpit and all fittings had gone. Apart from the building there was little to see but piles of boxes and crates and sack-covered objects which represented the museum stock.

"It doesn't look as if anything's happening at all." said Councillor Trelawney, staring into the roof beams.

"It'll take ages. It's a six-month job to catalogue and write up everything, what with cross references and books you can only get in the British Museum." Rowena shrugged.

"What *is* all that?" said Watts. "Specimens?"

"Yes. It's a folklore museum, as we explained."

"And folk *will* insist of calling up the devil at regular intervals," said Elfrida. "That's where your rumour came from, I'm sure."

Susan stopped as she came out of the wood. She heard a breathless little giggle from the sky and looked up sharply. For a moment she could not place the noise, then saw a pair of small legs dangling from the branch of an ash tree. The legs were fourteen feet up from the ground on the lowest branch of the big tree. She caught her breath.

"Darling! What are you doing up there?" Then she replaced shock with tension. "How did you get there?"

The child gabbled something to the branch he was sitting on.

"What? Now sit quite still, darling and tell me how *did* you get up there?"

He bent and she stood rigid hands out, frightened he would fall.

"My friend lifted me," he said and grinned so that for a moment the Cheshire Cat pushed its way into her head, and disappeared in its own grin.

She felt cold, stiff, every muscle still but the walloping of her heart.

"Your friend," she said, and tried to smile calmly. "I see. Well, you stay there and I'll get a ladder." The significance of "the friend" was stored in the back of her head unopened; her anxiety took up the whole of her waking brain.

She began to back away. "Don't worry, now. I won't be a minute. You stay there, there's a darling."

"I don't want a ladder!" he said with the superior clarity of confident youth. "My friend will lift me down. Don't you look. Turn your back. Don't look!"

She turned her back. "You won't try and get down, darling? Don't try and get down!"

"Don't look!" he screamed.

She hunched her shoulders, closed her eyes and shut her jaws tight. She felt it was the only thing she could do was to obey him because there was nothing else to be done, short of screaming for help and that would certainly make him fall off.

The seconds ticked by in months. She heard a dog barking on a distant beach. Her heart had stopped altogether so she could hear the rustling of young leaves.

"Darling?" she said in a strained voice.

Suddenly there was a small, evil chuckle right behind her.

"You can look now, Mummy!"

She turned, grabbed him and held him so tight to

her bosom he struggled in case he should be squashed.

Over his curly head she could see the tree, and the wood, and the grass, and the bluebells shooting in the young grass, and nobody there at all.

"I'm thirsty," said Gawain.

"Yes," said Susan breathlessly. "Yes, darling, we'll go and get a nice, cool lemonade."

They went home through the wood. Susan kept glancing quickly back, but the only moving life were birds swooping for insects low over the grass by the path.

2

Taking a look through the town this morning I was interested to see that no one seemed to be aware of the arrival of any alien visitors.

The people in the vicarage say nothing of what has happened to them. Talking of invisible things appears to be against rules, apart from a lot of hereditary talk and stuff about God. But from what I've seen in my visits, if any one of these people believed he had a visit from this invisible God, he would either say nothing for fear of being thought insane, or he would tell people and be certified insane.

All these little oddities are entertaining and I find them appealing, I suppose, because the Explosion carried so much of our mental work and hopes in it that some of the spirit of our lives went up with all the rest of the mess.

The insistence on material satisfaction for fear is almost universal. Here they want to see, on other earths they want to smell, or feel, or hear, and as long as they can place where the threat is, they seem to know what to do: usually, kill it.

Of course, the Old Man kills creatures. He's always killing them, but he makes a careful note of the numbers of sparrows, rats, elephants or dinosaurs, though he does not like hairless creatures as he has perfected a machine for counting hairs, and this he insists will be of great use for the next experiment. What that will be, I shudder to think.

Perhaps my fear of it is a small part of the reason why I took a little holiday. And I can always fill in my log with the word "Researches".

Meanwhile the life of the town goes on normally and nobody takes notice of the invasion ship under the bay, because nobody can see it so, even if they were told, I don't suppose it would cause much disturbance, unless for a few days they organised boat trips to try and find it, like the Loch Ness monster, which they haven't found in nearly fifty years. Which is fortunate for the poor fish.

3

At the RAF station by the estuary at 1105 the Air Vice Marshal heard that there had been no untoward tracks, sightings, soundings or smells of intruders since he had left, with the exception of three rabbits and a hare from the perimeter, all of which would be processed for game pie in the mess.

The officer saw the SMO at 1153. The doctor thought it a routine visit.

"I want an unofficial check-up," the officer said, smiling.

"Of course," the doctor said, relaxing into a grin. "You want Frankenstein?"

"It's the quickest, cleanest, easiest, yes."

The girl orderly showed him into the machine. He stood for three minutes and she smiled him out again. She went out to her office.

"It's top rate," the MO said, reading the print. "When did you have your regular check?"

"Eight months. Okay?"

"It's okay still." The MO sat back. "Worried about anything, sir?"

"Inflated," the officer said, "but confused. Last night I accomplished something I've never done in my life before, not even as a youthful enthusiast."

The MO cocked his head. "Yes?"

"I did three beautiful women, one after the other," the officer said.

The MO burst. "I'm sorry, sir. Congratulations! But why worry about that?"

"I'm fifty-two. My habits are smooth. Like brandy. Make it last. Don't rush. Then rest. Sleep. As the poet said, 'Bum to bum for the rest of the night'." He drew breath, enjoying it. "Last night I was consumed with inspiration. It was bloody unusual."

"You'll pardon me asking, but have you come here to boast?"

"I've come here because I don't understand it."

"Then let us come to the lead question. Did you enjoy it?"

"I was ecstatic."

"Well, leave it at that. The only thing I would say is, if you begin to lose weight, have another check. Oh, you didn't take anything before, sir?"

"I don't know of anything, even in mess room legend, that could have done that for me."

"There's just this. You wanted to? It was in your head? You fancied?" He sat back. "You did? Well, the only abnormality is you never did it before. That may be because you never had the luck before. I don't think you need a doctor. You need a thanksgiving service."

In the control room the Air Vice Marshal was told of a message received only minutes before.

"Some man in the town saw a saucer hovering above the church tower last night. It was circular, had orange lights and swooped up into the sky while he watched. He didn't report before because he was in the nick overnight and saw it through his cell window. He said it was his principle never to tell the fuzz anything, so he rang us when he got let out."

The officer glanced at the report. "Hang it in the bog," he said, "marked 'Secret – initial before disposing'."

In the Commanding Officer's room the visitor said, "Tom, do you believe in wild hunches?"

"There's a joker in every pack, man. The only trouble officially is you have to explain. But me, personally? Yes, I go for them."

"Even when you don't know where they come from?"

"Tell me what's on the hunch market this morning."

"Sometime last night I had the idea right in the back of my mind that there is something waiting out there." He pointed through the window.

"In the estuary?"

"No. The sea. I seem to remember the idea even placed it west of the headland. Couple of miles, say." He turned to the map covering the wall. "Perhaps we could get a Nimrod to make a strip search for practice, of course."

"That's an expensive hunch you have, sir. Thank God, it's not my pigeon."

The air officer thought a moment then looked out of the window again.

"Well I am here as a wandering dog's nose," he said. "If I get a scent I ought to be free to bark."

"The point is, old boy, we had a shade and that shade was corroborated apparently coming down but it died long before it got anywhere near here. Burnt out coming in, perhaps. Agreed it couldn't have been any of our orbiting dustbins because that would have given proper response. It might have been some space dust that disintegrated. Bit off a comet, anything."

"But none of the satellites picked it up. That's what's odd. It's possible it was some kind of craft carrying a protective beam against our finders and when coming down through our atmosphere, the beam went unstable for a second or two, then recovered."

"If it went down where you say, protected against

our probes as you assume, it should still have been sighted by the coastguards."

"I'm here because, back at the ranch, one of the Government quakers shook out of his shoes and got the idea that because there was nothing there must be something. It's a kind of logic up there. It's not what's happening but what isn't that counts."

"And have you spun round to the quivering view?"

"There was that light over the town last night and not all our piety nor wit made anything of it. It was a light, we saw it was a light, but our instruments gave no light trace, so there was no light scientifically; but we saw it.

"I stayed over there last night. An old vicarage, and there's something in the air there I can't explain. If it's haunting it's the most exhilarating ghost I ever came across. But I don't think it is anything like that."

"Forgive me opening old wounds, but at the beginning of your service career you gained the distinctive name of Crackpot Jones. I think Jones came from Casey the mad engine driver, but I *know* where the Crackpot came from. Are you, in your declining years, reverting to type?"

"What is the difference between a wild hunch and getting the quivers because nothing is there?"

"There is no difference. If I were you I'd have a go. Here's the direct blower. Call up Harry, but his Nimrods are on overtime. Still, you know that. The only thing worrying me is that if your phantom ship had a protective sensor belt against our probes, why do you think it's stopped using it now it's under the sea?"

"I had thought of that, but hoped that a search of

seabed levels might show up something. It is only a hope."

"You've been smoking that pipe all the time we've been talking and you haven't lit it yet. You must be dead keen on this hunch."

4

"You didn't see him lifted down?" Elfrida said eagerly.

"I dared not look. I promised. I didn't want him to watch me and then fall off. It was a hell of a way up, that branch. But next second, there he was down on the ground. Well, that proves it beyond doubt. There is something physical loose here."

"The councillor's bum also proves it," Rowena said. "I wonder what she'll spread around? On the face of it, they were on our side when they left, but they might say different amongst their cronies."

"Whatever it is, it's not a poltergeist or anything like that," Elfrida said firmly. "The whole history of such things is mischief, destruction, ill-wishing, evil. I never heard of one going around amusing the children, making them models, lifting them up trees and down again." She sat back. "It's out of this world. Really!"

"But what's this goosing business?" Susan said. "Is that his way of amusing the girls, or frightening them stiff?"

"It might be an international sign language for when he wants something," said Rowena. "It is, of course, but I meant universal. He's an alien. A bug-eyed bugger from a Black Hole."

"Facetious," said Susan sharply.

"He's pretty facetious himself, isn't he?" Rowena said. "So far, if he's real, he's a child-loving sex maniac. No, I don't mean about children, Sue, don't be silly. He's a womaniser. He might even think that by getting on the right side of Gawain he'll get round you. Ah!"

"Now that does sound sense," said Elfrida.

"Common sense," said Susan. "But there's a weakness. It makes him human."

"Or maybe that he understands humans," corrected Elfrida.

"We ought to tell the men, whatever happens," Susan said.

"Leo'll go rotten mad jealous," Rowena said. "You know what he is."

"Curious how well they both slept last night," said Elfrida as if thinking of something else.

"Don't let anybody feel a second's easy," Susan said.

"I never like people to feel easy when there is something to do."

"And what do we do now?" said Susan angrily. "Move?"

"Surrendering isn't doing something," said Elfrida. "It's just letting go of everything you've got that's worth anything."

"Talk, talk, talk!" said Susan.

"This is the age of talk, the final stage before absolute decay and rolling in compost over the edge of the abyss. Permissive society? What balls! All it does is talk too much about it. In my extensive experience I have found the boys who talk just can't do. Talk is a substitute. A fend-off. The peacock feathers for feathers that have no cock. I have the feeling that if—"

"Spare us the blurb for 'My First Two Thousand Fucks'," Susan cried out.

"It's true about the talkative ones, though," said Rowena. "And don't lose thatch, Sue, dear. We're all on edge. Just trying to find out what edge we're on, that's all."

"I was about to say that if we laid ourselves out for this Pan," went on Elfrida, unshaken. "he wouldn't have us. But is it worth trying? I mean, seducing the beast on his own ground?"

"Look," Susan said, "last night you think you went somewhere after he mauled you, but did he actually screw you?"

"I would say no," said Elfrida.

"You don't know?" said Rowena, surprised.

"I would say no again."

"We're not dealing with ordinary things," Susan said. "I have the idea that our guest knows something. I think that he came here because he knew that Pan was here."

Elfrida nodded in acknowledgment of her Pan idea being accepted.

"Well, he didn't take it very seriously, did he?" Rowena said, and laughed.

"You refuse to take this seriously!" Susan said.

"Well, look," Rowena said and sat very straight, "do you feel this Pan is a serious threat to you, us or anybody?"

Susan turned to Elfrida. "Do you?"

"It's the most interesting thing I've ever come across. I love it."

Susan looked at the table, then smacked both hands on it.

"I don't know what to make of it!" she said. "I feel I should," she lost her firmness and shrugged, "but I can't." She got up. "We've all got work to do, business to think about, and we're sitting here doing nothing, talking like a lot of idiot schoolgirls about a butcher boy we mustn't let mother know about. What in hell has happened?"

"It is the metamorphosis," said Elfrida, looking round.

"Let's get out of here for a bit. Take Gawain to the beach, have lunch at the Frigger's," said Rowena. "Then we can see how we feel when we're away from here."

All agreed, They got into Susan's car and drove over to the other town and the pub facing the sands, and played with the little boy, and had drinks and lunch, and walked about the narrow streets of the town and bought things, and talked to the fishermen, and went back on the sands and built sandcastles for the little boy, and talked about everything in the world except Pan.

After four hours they discussed what they wanted to do.

They all wanted to get back.

Six

1

They turned into the drive across the pavement and when they came in view of the vicarage round the privet hedge on the curve, Susan stopped. They all looked at the house except Gawain who had a small crab in his bucket and was watching it search round the plastic prison for a way out.

"Is something different?" Susan said. "With the house?"

"It hasn't moved, has it?" Rowena said.

"It can't have, can it?" Susan looked alarmed.

"I'm not so used to the view," Elfrida said. "It was dark when I came last night, but it does look different from what I saw in the moonlight. There is something."

Susan got out and looked; so did Rowena. Elfrida sat beside Gawain and looked in his bucket for a moment and made a joke so he giggled and nearly dropped the pail. She looked up again.

"I'm a stranger in these parts," she said out of the window, "but that tree wasn't there this morning. I am sure of that. The change makes it look as if the house has moved. That tree at the far end of the front beyond the Muck Room, or whatever it is."

Both girls looked. Susan snapped a finger.

"That's it!" she said. "Who moved it? Some sort of joke?"

She jumped back in the car. Rowena walked along the grass, cutting off the drive corner, and by the time the car had stopped and Susan and Elfrida got out, Rowena was already there.

The ash was halfway between the house wall and the wood, where the ground had been clear grass before. They all looked at the base of the tree, but the ground looked as if if had grown there from seeding, years before. There was no recent disturbance to be seen.

"Is it the one?" Elfrida said.

Susan looked up to the first thick branch, clenched her teeth an instant, then nodded.

"Yes, that's the one. This is a silly sort of a trick, isn't it? What's the point?"

Gawain ran up with his bucket.

"Mummy, it's a new tree!" He looked up it, grinning, then screwed up his eyes. "No it isn't, Mummy. He's brought it to me for a present! My friend!"

"That's nice," Susan said vaguely. "Let's go and have tea, shall we?"

"Can I play with it after?"

Susan looked away to the house wall. "Perhaps, dear. We'll see."

They went into the house. Rowena and Elfrida stayed looking down past the church to the white line of a hotel faraway across the estuary in its cliff of dark green.

"Looks like some kind of palace fallen over sideways in a moment of excess," Rowena said. "I said to my father once, how did I get this name? And he said unto me, what's the matter with it, and your mother liked it because she was romantic."

"I thought it was a Saxon queen," said Elfrida, "but Susan comes from the Saxon lands of East Anglia. You should change names. Susan must be Hebrew; Susanna was tried for her virginity or something. The Old Testament of Science Fiction shows she won against the Jewish elders and so virginity was established in the chronicles as a possibility, like going up in a chariot of fire."

"The tree," she added looking back at it, "has got to be a message."

"You must be worried," Rowena said. "You haven't lost yourself all day. Talking, I mean."

"I lose myself because normally I think of everything at once and they all push to get out first. Now I have one thing to think about, only one thing gets out at a time. The in-betweens are fill-ups; the commercials.

"I am sure my theory was right, about these fellows raiding for women."

"Well, if the women they take last seven thousand years, I'm not sure I want to go. It doesn't sound exciting, does it?"

"All you're doing is turning your back on the tree," Elfrida said.

"I don't want to know about the tree," said Rowena. "We've bought this place between the four of us and we like it, or we did till last night. I'm just going to think about something else till the tree goes back.

What we have is in this place; the shops are rented; this is *ours*. Now what's happening?"

"What do you mean, 'till the tree goes back'?"

An estate car came up the drive and stopped. The officer got out. He smiled then noticed the tree and came towards the women slowly, looking from them to the tree and back. They looked at him almost as if hoping he might do something about it.

"A recent arrival," he said, stopping. He looked at the ground, then up into the young leaves of the tree as they moved in the touch of a warm breeze.

"How did this—?" Rowena began.

He lifted a finger for silence, still looking up into the tree. He cocked his head. The women kept perfectly still.

He shifted his gaze from the tree branches to the women, then looked at the trunk and walked slowly forward and right through it. On the instant he appeared to come out beyond the trunk, the tree vanished.

He turned to them.

"Merlin," said Elfrida in admiration. "How did you know?"

"It's an optical trick, but I didn't know. The only thing was all the little leaves were moving in the wind, but there was no sound at all. I always think that for any small lively movement there ought to be a response, a chuckle in spring, a death rattle in autumn. This apparent tree was silent."

He looked into the wood.

"Do you know where the tree is?"

"I think its the one on the other side of the wood,"

Rowena said. "I'll show you. Gawain was lost up it this morning." She told the officer about the magic lifting of the boy as they went away through the woods.

Elfrida went into the house. Susan was in the hall. She looked round sharply.

"All illusion," the woman said. "Our friend walked through it and it vanished."

Susan stood still a moment, then, "Gone altogether?"

"It was never there."

Susan looked towards the kitchen. "He's having tea." She spoke softly. "I've been getting at him about what his friend looks like today." She shook her head. "He's never seen him."

"Sure?"

"All children have imaginary friends at one time or another," Susan said. "Gaw's had one or two before now. Well, now we know he's got a real - well, somehow real - one, but he's never seen him. He said it was a little boy with red hair and cherry-button eyes, if you can imagine what that is. That was this morning. Just now it was a little boy in a green suit and yellow hair." She shook her head again. "He's never seen anyone."

"Perhaps that's why he's not frightened."

"But it touches him and he's still not frightened."

"Yes, that is surprising. There is some considerable influence being used, but it seems itself to be childlike. Perhaps that's what appeals to a little boy."

"I feel I ought to take him away."

"Is there somewhere?"

"My parents." She shrugged. "But it's a hell of a

way. Means a couple of days, and I'm just not in the mood to leave here when all this is happening. Besides," she said, finding an excuse, "the last time I left him there for four days he came back rebellious, rude and unmanageable. I had absolute hell for a week after."

"The vicar spoils him?"

"The dear vicar is a bloody-minded old rebel himself. My mother fills the boy up with tarts and cakes until he's like a small balloon."

"So you don't want to send him away?"

"No." Susan sat on the wide stairs. Elfrida leant on the newel post. "I'm in a very odd mood. Last night unsettled me. It just left an empty excitement, as if I should be doing something quite different, something freer." She leaned back against the banisters.

"I know. I was married," Elfrida said. "A few weeks of fire, lust and passion, gradually dropping off into a regular exercise and you lie there and think, 'Oh God, is this all there is to it? Surely there's something more?' And you get the awful feeling that there isn't. Then you feel it can't be right, and that *he* is wrong, so you begin imagining a better him and find one and he's worse."

Susan laughed shortly. "Yes. Yes, I suppose it's general. Ro and I both got like that and talked about it, and other girls seemed to find something much the same, so then we decided on trying the swop business and that, of course, improved things for quite a while. We were, after all, all fond of each other."

"And it worked. It worked for a long time, really; began to be almost like a game. We shared everything, and then, sure enough, things all slowed down. I began to be frightened that two wasn't enough for me. I should have four. I was just a sex-bag, indiscriminate, a nympho. Then Gaw came and all was saved. Then, recently, I began to get the old itch, trying to find out if there was something new somewhere. And there is." She stayed, leaning back against the rails, staring at the wall.

"There always is," Elfrida said, looking away to the open door. "But when you find it, what will you do? Hold it? But that's what you always try to do, until you see there's something else further on, or was it behind somewhere? Or on the fork of the road you didn't take and always felt might be the way to Shangri La? So back; and when you get there: oh no, this wasn't it, not this at all. I must go back to the fork and try *again*, because it couldn't have been Shangri La but a hoarding telling about Shangri La and its multi-colour beauty. So back and back and off to the *right* of the fork and to the lake you've seen before; the lake with weeping willow and cherry blossom above and below the water, and you take the boat with no rudder, and paddle with your hands in sweet warm water, round and round: 'Surely this must be somewhere near where I caught the fish of Happiness? Or did I ever catch it?' And as the mist comes slowly, smiling pink across the water to take you, and the trees and shore have drifted into nothing, you hope that, somehow, it was all a dream, and you will wake and run back to what you could love and hold to you. But by then, there is no way back to the shore."

"Do I want to know the way back? I don't really

love anybody. I want to fulfil myself. I want just to see what me is supposed to be for, to—"

"Mummy, can I have some more sponge?"

"Please!" shouted Susan.

"*Please,* Mummy, can I have some more *sponge*?"

Susan suddenly relaxed and got up. "I'll cut you some." She went out.

Is that too little to be anything? Elfrida thought. But it is a part of everything. Sponge was built for me to buy when I thought of other people, for me to be pleased to give to my little son, to feed him, make him happy, convince him that I am kind, watching him, thinking of him. Surely nothing is too little. Or is it? Oh God, why am I here? Oh God why do I ask such stupid questions? Oh God, what am I? Oh God, does it matter if I know or not? Yes, it is worse if I know. Oh God, why can't I take what I am? But what am I, God? It's not God that made us think. It's what the Devil puts into ourselves over our shoulders. If we didn't keep thinking there must be something else, we'd be happy. If we didn't think, we'd be intelligent. That is because we don't think but pretend we do. Man thinking is like the little boy's imaginary friend. Pretend. And if I pretend there is nothing in this hall with me, there is nothing, and the hall is empty, and there is no one to be seen, so there is nothing.

But I know there is because that is not thinking, that is knowing.

Susan came back.

"They're a long time looking at that tree," she said.

Elfrida smiled. I am not jealous, you are not jealous, they are not jealous, because the man isn't mine, but he is because I felt he should be after once, and I am just interested why they are so long because I am jealous, but not much, because I have my husbands and if I want I can be very much liked and there is no need, but I am suspicious of why they are so long, and I am angry because they may be – what? Holding up tea, of course, holding up tea, keeping tea waiting, and we are not having tea until I have just thought of it, so they shall hold it up, and I am a little bit jealous and I want the man again, what nonsense, why should I? But if it so happens that he comes—

"Shall we have a cup of tea?" said Susan, and stopped Elfrida's tape rolling.

2

They looked at the tree.

"Elfrida is the thinker," Rowena said. "I mean, she tries to find out more than anybody else. Has she told you about last night?"

"Last night?" he said, quietly.

"I'll tell you," said Rowena, quickly. "She thought somebody was in the room when she was reading—" She told the rare adventure.

He stayed silent.

"Do you think there's any sense in this invasion thing she's dreamed up?" Rowena said, and then added hurriedly, "I don't mean her experience last night, I mean about what she's got from the books and the little lady figure."

"It's always hard to say," he said, looking at the tree.

"Suppose somebody wanted to invade. I was thinking of military things, you know," Rowena said, "would anybody choose this place?"

"To form a bridgehead?" he said, staring across the estuary. "Yes, depending on what weapons you had. All invasions depend on that. The old idea of firing a way in and blasting the enemy out merely results in each side losing. At the end, there is nothing to gain. The enemy retreats but the victor is left with a stinking plague-pit which he has to rebuild to save himself."

She knew he was talking to deflect her, and decided against pushing it. He kept looking across the estuary. He didn't look at her.

"But why worry yourself about things like that?" he said, turning back. "If there is an invasion from upwards, they might choose anywhere. It might not even matter to them where it was so long as it was a quiet place and there were quiet people, unlikely to be hostile."

He looked at her. She looked at him as if not quite sure what she wanted.

"I don't know why you're bothering about things like that," he said, hoping to help.

She leant back against the tree. "She said they were sort of oblongs, square-edged, standing up, transparent and pretty coloured. Now if you'd got to a stage where you'd got all your sensations out on – well, radio contacts so that you still got all the sensations of your senses – well, I mean, still enjoyed everything going on, but you didn't have to make it physically— Are you with me?"

"Yes."

"What shape would you choose, just to be the control box, as you might call it?"

"I wouldn't choose any shape. I'd sooner be dead. And if you turned oblong I'd say, 'Farewell, I'll always love you as you were, but to hell with the corners'."

She laughed. "I think you're sex-mad."

"I love women. Is that bad?"

"Oh, Cedric!" she said, holding out her arms.

"That's a hell of a name," he said.

"We've all got helluva names," she said. "It's because our parents thought more of the Old Ones who Did, rather than the New Ones, who Don't."

"You prefer the Vikings?"

"Carry me off and see." She laughed.

"Rowena," he said, frowning. "Is that to do with Rowan? Rowan was a name for the mountain ash, a tree that was supposed to ward off witches." He looked up the tree. "This is an ash."

"And how did it hurl itself over to the far side of the wood?"

"Visual transference. Perfectly blended in the scene; light, shadow, everything just right. Once had a course on interpreting photographs. One learns to notice lights and shadows." He frowned again. "It was so perfectly done. Almost alarming."

"If there was an invasion and you saw the enemy where it wasn't," she said, "you'd fire at the image, would you?"

"You are a thought reader, but there are far more dangerous situations than that. You see the hotel over there across the water? I booked dinner there for six forty-five. Is that all right?"

3

They dined on the veranda on the cliff overlooking the sea. The officer had thought of everything, including making sure there was a children's room with a nurse, so Gawain could fall asleep while they went on chatting in the sunset.

Arthur had had a busy day of travel, looking for interesting objects either to sell or put in the church museum. He so grumbled on his weariness that the officer began to see him covered in road dust carrying the despatch bag after having had to shoot his exhausted pony.

Leo had had a frustrating day of anger and shame. The noted author who had been engaged to sign his books for adoring fans in the shop, turned up drunk in a bath towel and turban, tried to seduce Mrs. Top Assistant - and had at one time got her trapped in the lavatory - and only gave in when the fire brigade was almost called to bust the door down. The local press was in the shop clamouring for pictures of the author, specially of the state he was in.

They got the final pictures when the author swept all the books off the main counter and laid down on it with the intention of levitating himself. The sudden appearance of rivulets running off the counter edges indicated levitation of the wrong sort. By that time the scoundrel was asleep and the shop had to be cleared and shut.

All these adventures and tribulations were related with such grumbled feeling that there was nothing the women felt they had to tell of their own day.

Or they felt that what they might have told was too

important to be mixed up with a drunken novelist wetting himself on a bookshop counter.

Both Leo and Arthur had come straight to the hotel as agreed by phone earlier, so the usual perfunctory questions and unheeded answers as to the day's affairs at home had been missed on Susan's part.

Susan, appreciating the convenience of having the nursery with nurse for dinner, began to think of having such a convenience at home so that she could go back to full participation in James, Marchant and Wives Limited.

Susan was very restless.

Rowena was bright and talkative. Elfrida was trying to answer Arthur's questions about the probability of certain purchases being early Phoenician bar stools. The officer talked to everybody on most subjects offered, making jokes of a lot of them. He was very popular.

Once he said, "Elfrida, you write books on your travels and discoveries. From small relics you build up pictures of long-gone civilisations. Do you find yourself building up pictures of everyday things you handle?"

"Yes. You pick up something, wonder who made it, how, what the material came from. That's quite normal."

"Suppose you wrote a book about the happenings in the vicarage in the last twenty-four hours? The clock striking. The light over the tower. The fairy influences in the air. Your travels in space?"

"In space?" said Arthur, turning to her. "You haven't been in space, have you? Or are you making something up? They don't have women up in those. Or is it something being kept secret? Oh, you're Air

Force. You'd know. But surely Elfrida—!"

"I would," said Elfrida, overriding Arthur, "work on the premise that this is the return of aliens who came to this earth seven thousand years ago."

"We had all that last night!" said Leo. "About the plasticine lady, you mean?"

The nurse appeared on the veranda and came to Susan.

"Would you come with me, Mrs. James? Your little boy is very, very restless."

The officer watched with particular interest as Susan got up and went away with the nurse.

The little boy has not brought his playmate with him, he thought. They are here. Other playmates. A flanking motion on Tom's airfield.

He looked over the veranda rail to the sea sparkling lazily under the sinking sun. In the distance he saw a dragonfly droning over the water towards the estuary. He recognised the attitude.

Harry's Nimrod is prowling at last, released from its capital duty of finding the Norwegian with the appendicitis forty miles west of the Scillies. What a life, combing the oceans for a Norwegian appendix who can't radio his position because he can't work it out, because his automatic pilot goofed off Kinsale while he slept in his bunk.

Suppose the aliens are ashore in numbers? How can that be found out?

He looked further south to the trees leading off the headland, the falling ground going down towards the town on the water and the solemn finger of the church tower pointing in warning at the calm sky.

It did not look possible that any invasion could be happening in the almost motionless scene, but that was how a perfect invasion ought to look; as if nothing was happening.

What do the defenders do? Find the hosts of Valhalla invisibly probing the weaknesses of the fabric for an easy way in? How?

"I remember Mrs. Dollboys kicking up a fuss about that Jacobean table because her husband told her Cromwell had had a lot of imitations made to debase the currency," Arthur was saying through his cigar.

"You're getting to the point of talking as much intolerable cock as your customers," Leo said.

"Balls," said Arthur, in a casual tone. "What do you think, Ro?"

"I wish I'd gone in today," she said. "Look what I missed. I could have been chased into the lavvo instead of Lil."

"He was too pissed to achieve," said Leo. "You missed nothing. Besides, darling daughter was panting to get into the bog with him instead of her Mama, so you wouldn't have won."

It isn't sex that springs us, but just the sudden delight of something surprising, something jumping the rails that makes our insides leap up for joy, the officer ruminated. Last night inspiration from the stars had I, today the pancake thoughts of a weary old time-server, just wishing I could do it all over again; but how I invented it all last night I shall never know and shall be for ever grateful. I wonder if I could do it all over again? I think I could love myself for ever, retiring in confidence, never wanting more.

Susan came back.

"It has been lovely," she said, "but Gawain is playing hell for the nurse. Could we hurry the brandy?"

"Fetch the wee hogs-pudding," Leo said. "We won't be five minutes."

It had not struck Leo that Gawain's troubles might be his playmate. Filled with the troubles of his day, Leo was thinking mostly of himself. His father was a Viking man, after all. "Don't worry about women," father always said. "Give 'em children and get dressed for the next hunt."

Arthur, the officer had noticed, had had a very hard day and his dust of the road was not streaked with sweat, but whisky. Buying rarities from strangers for too little is a difficult business, when the affair usually ends in the sucker giving Scotch to the mugger in gratitude for rape.

As if thought-reading, Arthur pointed his cigar at the officer and said, "I never collect the stuff at the time, you know. Send the van a couple of days later. They think I'm honest if I do that." He smoked again with the slowness of comfortable conscience.

"When we get back," said Rowena. "I'll give you Irish coffee." She smiled at the officer. "I'll borrow some cream here."

She beamed, pleased not only with the thoughts of the future, but in warm recognition of her husband's successful day.

Elfrida sucked slowly at her cigar, then trailed smoke upwards from pursed lips at the ceiling.

"I prefer it *au naturel*," she said, and laughed at the officer. "Milk. In Surabayo we found a baby orangutan. When I cuddled it, it kept trying to get at my nipples. Do you think we are all different, or is there something all mammals recognise, no matter what it's attached to?"

"I don't usually bother with orang-utans," said Rowena cheerfully. "I was brought up in a brokers' belt, a different sort of jungle."

"Sometimes I wish I'd stayed on the farm," said Leo, with a drift to reminiscence. "But I couldn't get on with father's off-hand manner with animals. I like to love everything, not live on it. What's that aeroplane doing out there? Fly fishing?"

"A practice flight," said the officer. "Twilight is very good for practice. Changing light, you know. Instruments are not always the answer. And instruments need instruments to spy on instruments, and if the mother supply fails, all taps are stopped and then the pilot has to work out the simple problem, 'If I let this go on I shall drown in the bloody ocean if I survive the crump in the first place; so I shall pull back the column and sod the mechanicals and clump on home with my eyeballs stuck to the windscreen'."

"Poetic to the point of ultimate," said Leo. "I must have breathed too much of that literate piss artist," he shook his head, "I feel muff happy. What was that wine we had?"

"You stopped on the way," said Rowena. "I never knew you come home without stopping on the way."

"Excuse," Leo said. "I'd better tip the nurse. Lord knows what the boy did to her." He went.

"My memory is not good," said Elfrida. "I depend on my diaries to find where I was when something happened and when it was. I have to go to them because I'm such a liar. Or poetic, as Leo says. I like to drift on in my mind, making things up. It's when I try to argue I get so muddled."

"That's because you argue just to get something out of somebody else," said Arthur, his eyes half shut. "God! What a day! I've bought five items and listened to ten tragic life stories. My path has been strewn with wet hankies. It's against my nature.

"The primrose path, the primrose path,
I want to follow the primrose path,
And then I'll tiddly toddly tum,
Iffidy boffidy buggery bum."

"Most impressive," said Rowena. "The working day is pouring out of you, darling."

"I was indiscreet," he admitted. "One dear lady gave me some dandelion wine. She had made dandelion wine for years for her dear dead husband, and they'd been so happy and it had cured all their marital troubles and made life happy and all things possible, this bloody dandelion wine. You know how sentimentally weak I am. I drank some. I haven't landed yet. I don't think I will today. I shall land in the morning in a clanging of dustbin lids and my lower jaw wobbling on wires."

"Drink raw egg in raw Worcester sauce before you go to bed," said the officer. "It blows the head right off, lets the fresh air scour round the inside and then it comes back on, like a good dog. Tomorrow, you'll be sane."

Apparently idly, he watched the Nimrod flying up and down over the sea.

Susan came back. "Leo's taken him out to the car."

The officer looked up. "His friend?"

"His friend was there," Susan said, and laughed a little. "Nurse was very surprised. She thought it was my little boy who was feeling her when her back was turned, but each time she turned round to catch him he was dodging about somewhere else."

The officer watched the Nimrod as if trying to think of a question to ask. Arthur screwed his head half round and squinted up at Susan.

"What do you mean, ducks? Feeling her what?"

Susan realised that so far, the men had not heard about the amorous activities of the visiting Pan. It was no time to start penetrating Arthur's mental fog.

"Oh, just digging her in the back, you know," she said. "Being naughty. You know how he gets when he's excited."

"Like his father. Loose hands," said Arthur, comfortably and immersed himself in smoke again.

Later outside, it was noted with relief that Arthur had not driven to the hotel but had come with Leo, who proposed to drive him home.

"I want to drop off at the pub," Arthur said, leaning on the car roof as if about to make a speech about the imminent collapse of the universe.

"What, more?" said Rowena.

"Not drink, sweetness. Not that at all. I picked up a quite splendid Elizabethan side table and you know fishface is going to turn his stable barn into a dining room, so commerce, *Verstehen sie*?"

"In that case, Leo, you'd better go in with him and

hold him up," said Rowena, briefly. "We'll go back together."

"I shall get a hundred off the spiny bugger," said Arthur in dignified justification of his proposal.

"He might drink himself sober," said Susan. "That's one of his gifts."

It was dusk when the officer drove them up to the vicarage. Everyone was in a pleasant mood and getting on together in high spirits. Gawain had dropped off to sleep as he didn't understand the jokes, anyway.

"I'll take him," Rowena said. "You've got the keys, Sue."

Sue unlocked the door, stepped in, switched on the overhead lights, then stood quite still.

"What's the matter?" Elfrida said.

She stepped beside Susan and Rowena joined them, holding the sleeping child like a slack-jointed doll. The officer stood back, listening to the tense sounds of amazement. There was, he noted, no sound of fear.

"I'm sorry," Susan said, going in at last. "I was taken aback. Look at this!"

They all went in and stood around where the doormat should have been.

The great hall, empty and half painted as it had been when they went, was now richly furnished by a raving lunatic.

All the antique furniture which had been stacked in the Bishop's room and other store rooms upstairs had been brought into the hall and set in the profusion of a wooden jungle.

A collection of chairs, stools and two benches was lined up the stairs, lurching like tombstones because the treads were not deep enough to take the four legs of any chair. The middle of the floor was taken up by a heavy black oak chest with a copper coal bucket on top, sprouting the futurist flora of a set of golf clubs. A Dutch dresser stood around like a lost island, its shelves loaded with wine, Scotch, washing-up liquid, lavatory cleaners, gin, and fly-spray.

Susan began to walk slowly around the exhibits, bewildered.

"Welcome to Bedlam," Rowena said, and carried Gawain round the back of the dresser and in at the Glory Hole door where she laid the little sleeper on the sofa and pushed a couple of chair backs against it so he shouldn't fall off.

"There is a system," Elfrida said. "You see the chairs on the stairs. Now the watcher knows we sit on chairs, and he has seen Susan sitting on the stairs, so connection is made; he puts the chairs on the stairs.

"A dresser he has seen in the kitchen, with bottles and plates milling around on it, so as long as it's a bottle, up it goes on the shelves. Flowers in the vase, well, you must admit the clubs do look a bit like a spray of bent bullrushes."

"It must have taken hours," said Susan.

"It must have taken more than one," the officer said. "Might I use the phone? A routine call. It won't be charged."

He went into the office and came back shortly after.

"I'm afraid your line has been changed," he said.

Rowena said, "How changed?"

"It's been made a hot line to the station across the estuary."

"Do you mean we can't ring out?" said Susan blankly.

"Only to the station duty officer, and nobody else. I asked where the order came from. The officer said he didn't know. There is a written order on the duty officer's desk which came on the teleprint, *in code*. I have asked for the order to be traced. He'll ring back."

"But they've no right—" Susan said furiously.

"I don't think it's to do with us," the officer said in an odd tone. "I believe it's to do with," he indicated the mad museum with his hand, "with this lot."

"But how could they mess about with the phone line?" Rowena said. "That's the Post Office, the exchange— Do you mean they've just cut our line out and joined it straight across there?" She pointed out of the open door.

"It must have been done through the exchange. Where is it, do you know?"

"Oh, right over the back here. It's an automatic thing. I don't think there are people working in it."

"Far over the back?"

"Oh no. Over our back wall almost. A quarter of a mile? Maybe less."

Rowena looked at the mess in the hall, then turned to the door.

"I'll get that Irish coffee," she said, and fetched the borrowed cream from the car.

Elfrida sat on the black chest and rearranged the clubs, making them look more like flowers.

"You can forget any cross thoughts about hauntings, poltergeists and all the rest of it. This is physical. This is the sort of thing sometimes done by primitive people to make a relative believe the ghosts are after him, so he'll die and leave them his cattle. It's that sort of joke, which can be lethal if you're simple.

"This is just a much later development. It might be a demonstration of wishing to be helpful, friendly. It might be the opposite; to show us they're here and need to be reckoned with.

"Here we have a demonstration of their ability to watch us, note what we do, and connect one thing with another but without understanding exactly why we want these things. Perhaps they've gone ages beyond needing furniture, bottles, decorations. If they are blocks, as I saw, they don't need furniture at all."

"I agree," said the officer, "but the matter of the phone line is very different. They do understand that very clearly, and they know the system we use so they can fix it their way."

"I suppose you would call that a military development."

"In reverse," he said. "The usual system is to cut off communications to the enemy. But it does seem possible that your idea of an invasion could be right. But what has given rectangular blocks a need for women?"

Elfrida smiled. "Fancy me overlooking that."

Susan came from the Glory Hole. "Could you give a hand to clear a way up the stairs? I must get him to bed. He's dog tired."

"We could clap our hands and say, 'Put it all back where you found it!'" said Elfrida. "And then wait."

Rowena appeared from behind the dresser.

"Do that," she said, "and then we'll all go into the kitchen and shut the door."

Elfrida laughed.

Susan said, "*What?*"

The officer said, "Wilco."

So, in an odd atmosphere of well-humoured fear, uncertainty and bravado, they went into the kitchen. Susan went through into the Glory Hole. Gawain was sleeping.

"You say it, Elfrida," Rowena said. "You know him better than anybody."

She went into the hall and closed the door behind her. She looked up the staircase, then to the front door, still open, then all around. Then she looked at the stairs, shut her eyes, clapped her hands and so, "Put it back where you found it. Put it back. Back! Upstairs!" She made a circular motion with her finger, embracing all the stuff down in the hall, then pointed up the stairs. "Put it back!"

She opened the kitchen door and backed in, almost pushing over the eager girls inside.

"You didn't say, 'Please'," Susan said, and snorted over a little laugh.

Rowena filtered coffee into a jug, paying strict attention to what she was doing. The officer stood looking out of the uncurtained window at the wood, silhouetted against the brightening silver of the sky. Elfrida put her cigarette case open on the table and decided not to smoke one.

"Do you really think it will?" Susan said, turning from the door.

"I don't really think anything," said Elfrida. "I'm getting past think stages. I don't think I'm equal. But give everything a chance once."

Rowena turned. "A fault in the reasoning," she said. "All the bloody whisky is out on that dresser, and if he puts it all back where he found it, he's going to come in here."

"You're faulting his reasoning," said the officer. "If he wants to please, he won't barge in here."

"It's a hell of a test for the poor darling," said Elfrida.

"But I must have whisky," said Rowena impatiently. "It's my special gift, making this stuff."

The officer kept taking mental note that amongst the three women there was tension, excitement, even a sort of giggly pleasure over it all, but no real fear.

Susan pointed out. "There was some Irish out in the old larder. You put it there last time you did it."

"What? Whiskey with an 'e'?" said Rowena. "Joy, oh joy. That is the exact recipe." She went and got it, came back and arranged the glasses.

The room, with four people in it, was unnaturally quiet. They could hear the deep, satisfied breathing of the infant through the open door.

They sat down round the table. Rowena handed out her mixture after bidding the officer to watch her pour cream over the back of a silver spoon.

As they sat, all agreed the coffee was lovely and went on straining to hear if anything moved in the hall.

"Perhaps he'll wish it all up," said Rowena.

The officer began to laugh at the table top. "Sorry," he said. "You are like children waiting for Santa."

Then there was a crunch; a noise like some heavy wooden piece being dragged across the wood-block floor in the hall.

The officer jumped up and turned to the door. Elfrida grabbed his wrist.

"Don't!" she said.

He stayed still a moment, as if he had not heard, and then relaxed and leant on the back of his chair, head cocked, listening.

There were more grunts of scraping wood, bumps, thumps and more regular sounds of things being dragged, bumping up the stairs.

Susan felt her forehead and leaned back against the open door.

"I don't want to be frightened, but it's - horrible."

"It's unusual," Elfrida said, with bright eyes. "But they are doing what we asked. They are *doing* it. You can hear them doing it now!"

"All the same, it's creepy," Rowena said, hunching her shoulders to stop a shudder.

"Only because you can't *see* them," Elfrida hissed. "And remember, all they've done is be friendly. Everything they've done is friendly. Even putting the tree image out there. Perhaps Gawain asked for it to be nearer his room, or said he wished he could take it."

The noises went on for three minutes, and then there was silence beyond the kitchen door. They waited a minute or two after quiet fell, and then Rowena went to the door, opened it and looked out.

The hall was as clear as it had been earlier but for a range of bottles and containers which were formed up like troops on the floor in front of the kitchen door.

She laughed suddenly from pressure of nerves and at the silly apparition of the bottle troops.

"Look at this!" she said.

Seven

1

Mr. Watts was a conscientious councillor. When asked to investigate a place in the interests of the people, he would make sacrifices to be sure that he carried out his duties properly.

On the previous night, unable to sleep from frustration caused by Mrs. Watts's headache, he had got up, dressed and gone out into the fine night with his dog on a lead. His mind had been concerned with the public matter of the fate of the people's church, which drew his steps that way. He went from the pavement into the churchyard and along the side of the building. It was a peaceful night, beautiful, and his mind was very restless and might even have turned to black magic and devils prowling had he not, in the distance, seen a beautiful naked woman dancing in the moonlight.

He had watched for quite a while, suffering acute longings and excitements which he had fancied nature had cooled off for him.

In the end it was the dog getting impatient and pulling and threatening to bark that had made him go before he was discovered.

His restlessness and general demeanour had been affected the following day so that Councillor Trelawney, who had noticed before that his primness was mainly a guise, had seen his urgency in one or two small differences and so naturally suspected that later, when the interview began, it was he who had been making amorous advances by way of her curvaceous bottom.

Councillor Watts went through the day feeling the suppressed excitement of a man who has attained a secret lover, which aroused his emotions unwisely and Councillor Trelawney and Mrs. Hanson, Committee Secretary, had had cause to push him off and even smack his hand.

"I think," Mrs. Hanson whispered, "the worthy Watts has been taking pep pills."

That night Mrs. Watts had another headache and went to bed early. Mr. Watts decided to go for a walk and took the small pair of binoculars usually kept for walking holidays in Wales.

Thus it was that in a fever of expectation, he stationed himself in the graveyard and kept a look-out on the house. Having met the dancer herself that very morning made his condition far worse than it would have been, and he watched the open door of the house very sharply.

It was different from the night before as then, the place had looked empty; now it looked as if furniture removers had dumped their load in the hall.

He saw no one, but was prepared to wait. The night was again warm and moonlit; a very fine spell for May. It struck him that if he rested his elbows on the top of

Jeremiah Couch, Esq. of this parish, he would have a steadier hold on his binoculars. He tested the position on top of the tombstone and directed his glasses at the open front door.

He saw a heavy chest lift itself off the ground, swing uncertainly in the air and then project itself at the staircase.

Bewildered, Mr. Watts readjusted the glasses and looked again. There were a lot of chairs and things on the stairs, but as the chest started to go up, these articles hoisted themselves up to the top and out of the way.

Mr. Watts swallowed. His mouth was suddenly dry. His face felt wet. He wiped his forehead with a handkerchief, still holding the glasses with one hand so he could see.

One thing after the other lurched and hoisted itself up the stairs, even a great black dresser.

"God Almighty!" he whispered.

He wiped his face. Sweat was running into his eyes and spoiling the view. He watched again until the hall was emptied.

"It is black magic, of course it is! The rumour was correct," he whispered and wiped his face again. "Good God! Devil's neighbours!"

He turned then and went back down the steps to the church path alongside the building. He walked quickly in the shadow towards the corner, beyond which the yard joined the pavement. He turned the corner, still walking very quickly.

He stopped and looked about him. He had turned the corner but was still on the path at the side of the church. He looked back and to the right and there was the white vicarage up amongst the trees.

He thought he was mistaken, that his wish to get out of the place had made him think he had walked when he hadn't.

He started again, walking fast to the East corner of the church and turned round it.

And again he found himself walking down the path along the side of the church; again he looked back and saw the vicarage up amongst the trees.

His handkerchief was getting wet, but he used it again.

Something was happening to him, but he could not make out what.

He looked down towards the east corner once more; beyond that he knew there was the yard and the town pavement. This time he ran to it and turned the corner, then stopped again.

He was on the path at the side of the church and the vicarage was still up there amongst the trees.

He sat down on top of the little stone wall that held back the slope of the graveyard. He thought he would burst into tears like a little boy lost. He held his damp handkerchief to his mouth, shut his eyes and told himself he was awake and real and solid, and everything was as it should be.

Somewhere in the back of his head came the memory of a cautionary Sunday-school teacher telling him, "You will go blind and dizzy and not know what you are doing if you take to lascivious satisfactions in the mind."

Watts stood up. "Balls!" he shouted in defiance. "I

am *here*!" He thumped himself on the chest. "I am me and I am here! I am William Sebastian Watts, builder of this town, established 1878, Limited for tax purposes and councillor for twelve years, married, no issue but headaches, one collie dog named Rupert, and a cat. I am me, and I shall walk out of this bloody churchyard or die in the attempt. No. Perhaps not. I will walk out and no one shall stop me, not devils nor demons nor succubi nor concubines. Bugger the lot of you, I am going!"

He got up and walked firmly and without malice to the corner where he came softly and firmly into contact with Councillor Trelawney, who was rounding the same corner.

"Bill! Good God! What's the matter with you? I heard you shouting. Are you all right? I was just going down to the square for my car and I heard you. I thought, My God! That's Bill in extremis, or nearly. What *are* you doing?"

He stared at her; without a hat, she looked quite young in the moonlight, and might even dance if encouraged, and he said, "Meg, Meg! I've been brain damaged, or something. Thank God you've come. I was tipping my balance. Listen to me," he raised a finger and pointed over her shoulder at the cornerstone. "I have seven times walked round that corner and been walking in the same place! I have been round that *coin* eight times, nine times, and every time I've been walking in the *same place*!"

"Bill, sit down a moment," she said firmly, and watched while he sat back on the little wall again. "Are you well?"

"I don't know, Meg," he said, trying to rest his fevered head on her bosom and being pushed off until more was known. "The bloody place is bedevilled!"

She looked back at the corner of masonry, so solid and impartial, then back at Mr. Watts.

"What do you mean, back in the same place?" She turned to have a fuller look at the edge of the building. "Well, it's the same as it always was, the path goes round the corner and the little wall goes round the corner and the moon is shining on the big wall further on. There's no one there. Stop it, Bill." She swept an impatient hand behind at what she thought was his and hit nothing. "Will it help if I go with you? Let's try, shall we? We'll go together."

She held her hand out to him. He kissed it almost fiercely and got up, holding it tight. They both turned towards the corner of the building.

"Right. Come on," said Councillor Trelawney.

They walked. They turned the corner. They walked on, down along the side of the church. They stopped together. She looked all round. He just looked at her.

She was firm and angry. "Come on. We are going round that corner!"

She marched. He was almost dragged in her wake, until he caught her speed. They went round the corner and then were walking down by the side of the church again.

She stopped dead. "Shit!" she cried.

"What is it, Meg? What is it?" he said, cuddling her arm for more than comfort.

She looked at the corner, she looked up at the church

roof, then round to the placid moonlit face of the vicarage up amongst the trees.

"We must go up there," she said, threateningly. "They may know something!"

"I'm grateful to you, Meg," he said, wiping his face again. "I thought I was going off my head!"

"I think *I* am but I'm not going to admit it yet," she said, and led the way up the path between the lurching tombstones and through the garden to the big white house.

On the way he wondered whether to mention he had seen the furniture walking about in the house, but thought she might think he had been drinking. He was very uneasy and wanted no part of somebody else's frustrated anger to be turned on his small weaknesses as something that could be clobbered where larger events couldn't.

He was an indomitable coward.

"So sorry to barge in at this time of night, but we've just had the most appalling experience. Bill - Mr. Watts here - was shouting because he couldn't get out of the churchyard."

"I was going through to take a walk on the headland! Or coming back; rather I was when I couldn't—"

"I was just going down to get my car off the park - I was at the Conservative meeting this evening - when I heard him shouting to be let out. Well, I just thought the gate was shut and went to see what was the matter, and he said he couldn't, and when we tried together, *we* couldn't!"

"Couldn't *what*?" said Susan.

"Walk out of the churchyard! Every time we tried we came back to the same place! And we went and tried again, and on, and on, and gasp and pant, and on, and on again and again. Oh dear, oh dear."

The officer stood in the open kitchen door listening carefully, definite pictures beginning to form in his mind as to what was afoot in this area.

2

I see there is now a considerable activity in the ship under the bay. There are quite a number of the crew ashore and if the look-out keeps ringing this bloody bell every time I move I shall be constrained to reduce it and the ship as well, to rubbish. They bid fair to interrupt my studies of the humankind, the results of which I will enter in my log in the hope that when I return, the Old Man will agree I have spent my time in valuable pursuits.

I am grateful to the visitors for having led me back to this little place, but now they are becoming a nuisance, and I am not at all in favour of their preparations for making serious inroads into the peace of the place. I do not wish to take sides - the Old Man always accuses me of taking sides - but I am studying *humankind* at the moment and don't wish to be disturbed by a horde of Philodons coming up out of the sea. Besides, their women are very ugly.

3

At the time that the bewildered, angry councillors arrived at the house, Leo was driving Arthur out of the pub car park and round to the right, past two old shops to where the high wall of the vicarage grounds began. He flashed to turn right into the gateway, then cancelled and drew up, staring across the empty road at the wall.

"Where's the bloody gate?" he said.

"You're pissed," said Arthur, sunk low in the seat and richly smoking yet another cigar. "You've passed it."

For a moment Leo looked back at the shops, just to make sure he hadn't driven a distance without noticing. He drove slowly on, knowing he hadn't passed the gate and also knowing it should have been there when he flashed to cross the road.

After a minute or two, Arthur sat up. "What's the matter, chum? You've passed it, you twit. This is coming up to the corner!"

"Look back."

Arthur craned his neck. The lights from the town square shone on the long wall right down to the shops. There was no break in it.

"Some buggers must have blocked it in!" Arthur said. "Our gate! I'll have the knackers off them when I find who they are!"

"Nobody could have done it without the break showing," said Leo, with a tight-drawn mouth. "There's no break showing."

"Then we must be drunk," said Arthur, still staring through the back window.

Ahead the corner of the wall showed at the entrance to Petter Lane. Leo flashed and turned right into the lane. Slowly they drove down the lane. The long, unbroken wall with trees overhanging, ran beyond the range of the headlights.

"Of course, madam," chanted Arthur, "it was originally the Manor House and the vicar had that ruined place down the far end, and all we ask for this charming property is three hundred and forty-five thousand quid, most of it on deposit."

He looked at the telephone exchange on the left of the lane, set back amongst trees, windows dim lit, glowing like a robot's eyes.

Further on, Leo stopped.

"There's no back gate," he said, pointing across the road.

Arthur opened the door and got out. The moon was bright but the opening leaves of the trees overhanging the wall cast it in shadow. He crossed the lane and looked at the wall, across one way and then the other.

"Shine the lights here," he said.

Leo backed, then turned the car across the lane, lighting the wall for some distance. Arthur looked at the ground, but there was no sign on the road edge or in the little ditch to indicate that there had ever been a turn-in.

"We are crapped," he said. "Life is neither real nor earnest," He went back to the car and got in. "Well, if we now have no gates, due to some high-speed joker of a wall builder, how shall we get in?"

"We'll go on to the common, park and walk back through the churchyard," said Leo. "I don't fancy climbing this wall."

"There's enough ancient broken glass up on top there to satisfy Agrippa, the cabin boy," said Arthur. "No, leave the wall." As Leo started again, "I tell you a good cure for alcoholic fumes. This bloody lot. My head is now as clear as a bell and I have no idea what to do with it. It recognises no part of this miracle." He looked at Leo. "Unless it's *us*."

"If it's us, then we'd better drive on to the looney bin, because my orientation is going like a humming top. But it isn't us. Something is happening. You must admit the girls were a little bit odd this evening."

"I didn't notice enough to admit it."

"And that Air Force chap. He was thinking about something else, and when the nurse came in he more or less dived into it. The plasticine woman; the burglar, or whatever he was, and all that kerfuffle in the night; Elfrida and her books and getting fey and then at dinner—"

"At dinner he kept looking at that plane droning up and down over the sea. It was something to do with him. As if he was waiting for what it would find—"

"And talking of this airborne crap pot," said Arthur, "let us be back to where you said you were going to go, not out into the wilderness. We're past the end of the lane."

Leo said, "Are you off your tiny nut? We haven't turned out of the lane yet!"

"If Jesus was driving, I wouldn't believe it. We are heading across the grass, going for the bloody cliff!

Joke's over, mate! Throw out the anchors!"

"I don't know who's supposed to be joking." Leo bawled. "At the end of this lane I turn right. Right?"

Arhtur looked at the front of the car heaving itself over the grassland towards the very top of the head. He raised his fists, seeing there were only yards before they went over the top and down on to the rocks on the beach.

"Stop the bloody juggernaut!" he shouted. "Joke's gone stale!" The cliff was suddenly too near. "Christ, you lunatic!"

He grabbed the wheel and pulled it round to the left. The car started to obey, then the back swung out over the grass and skidded. Arthur was in no position to correct the slide, concerned only with avoiding the clifftop and holding the wheel pulled left. Leo was trying to pull it back in order to avoid crashing into the lane ditch which wasn't there.

The car went over the cliff edge broadside, and turned over as it fell.

4

The officer said, "Please wait here. I would like to look into it. It could be a service matter." They all watched him as he went out.

He walked fast, down through the gardens, the graveyard, on to the side path of the church. Three times he walked to the corner and each time found himself back where he started.

"A development of the optical trick with the ash tree," he told a gravestone as he went back to the drive before the house.

At the drive he turned left and walked to the end. The moon painted dappled shadows on the drive surface and clearly showed its dead end up against the high brick wall.

The officer went to the wall, put out a hand and touched it. He felt solid brick, rough surfaced, with pointed mortar joints all round it. A solid wall which had not been there two hours before.

This was much more than just an optical trick. He stood for a moment looking at the wall where the gate had been, then closed his eyes, waited a few seconds, then walked slowly forward. He made several paces, then stopped and opened his eyes.

He stood on the edge of the pavement outside the wall.

He looked up and down the road and saw nobody. He turned and looked back at the wall. The perfect psychological trick. You see something you think is solid, touch it, and feel what your eyes have already decided is there.

Shut your eyes and see nothing. Expect to meet a solid wall but not *when*. Don't see *when* you appear to hit the wall and no wall exists.

He stood for a minute or more, thinking of the military consequences of such an invention.

What use are bombs and bullets when you can take the whole body of men prisoner with something that isn't there? Even if they know the trick and are taught to ignore it, you cannot really ignore something which you can see, feel, hear and smell.

You may use the eye-shut principle, but an army with its eyes shut is a pretty useless instrument, particularly when the enemy knows when the eyes will be shut. And you cannot train a battalion to walk into walls with their eyes shut. Nearly all walls *are* there.

One could fire at the wall and watch for the result, and that would give away your position and waste ammunition.

But such small practical considerations mattered nothing against the true purpose; that of showing the fighting man he has no control over his senses, and nobody fights in such a condition.

Furthermore, the officer felt certain, these tricks were clearly only part of a bagful of completely alien jiggery-pokery.

He faced the wall, took care not to think about the distance and walked back into the grounds again.

He turned for the last time, looked at the wall, judged the distance at three paces, shut his eyes and walked into it. It felt like any other wall, immovable by the human frame.

"It'll be joyous making out a report on this one," he said, and laughed as he went back to the house.

When he went in, the people all stopped talking and looked at him.

"You are right," he said. "There is some extra-sensory trickery going on round here."

"Black magic!" cried Meg Trelawney.

"That would be simple," the officer said.

The phone bell started to ring.

"That's got to be for you," Rowena said, sharply.

"I'm sorry," he said. "It's not my doing."

5

He stood at the desk looking down at the spread of magazines, sale catalogues, art reviews and shifted the phone cord slightly so as not to obstruct the cover of a review depicting the nude princesses with one pinching the other's nipple.

"There was definitely a siting by the Nimrod," the station commander said. "Some difference in the sea bed. The computers in the plane put it at three miles due west of the headland light, but a check computer overrode that and placed it two miles west of the first siting, that is four point eight nautical miles 287 degrees from the lighthouse. On landing at St. Mawgam, the station computer there ran the tapes and gave a position seven miles north-west of the light, on a bearing 329 degrees. It's easy to see on the map the discrepancies."

"Yes," said the officer, cocking his head at the princesses.

"The tapes and all available gen were flown over here by helicopter. We have run the original tapes through our computer which gives the position of the siting as six point seven miles south-west of the light on a bearing of 248 degrees. From this you will see that the computers are being ballsed up by some alien method, which amounts to us being peed on from a great height."

"That is not a humorous quotation; that is what is happening," the officer said. "We are being played with. Are your outside phone lines okay?"

"I suppose so. I'll get a check. So the Nimrod does

confirm something unusual but not where it is. I think we should request a Navy search. Echoes might be clearer on the surface. The most we could make of what it is down there is a heap of frayed wool, reaching about in all directions, edges moving with the currents, a nebulous shadow of sweet bugger all."

"Is there anything physically unusual in your camp? Walls where they shouldn't be?" The officer expanded and explained.

"I'll take a run round myself," the commander said. "Hold on, here's the signal report on the phones. They appear to be normal but the duty officer has doubts. He said the reply from London at this hour was too polite. He should know."

"It's encouraging in one sense that these people, wherever they're from, are almost as old-fashioned as we are, messing about with electronics. If that's what they're using for these optical tricks the problem may be as stiff as it seems now."

"Hold on." Another pause. "A signal from the Ministry. It advises, 'Message noted; priority following day'. That surely must be genuine. A put-off job."

"You could press the red button."

"I'd be shot. We've nothing concrete. What's happening? A blink exercise. We're being played with. Invasion? You may be right but it doesn't sound dangerous. Has anyone ever thought of a peaceful invasion? Why are all aliens bug-eyed muggers?"

"There was a Trojan Horse," said the officer, flipping the pages of the magazine. He stopped flipping and looked at a picture. "And, come to think of it, Delilah. Get yourself destroyed with lust."

"She was predictable. I never did think much of Samson. You say there is an illusion of being imprisoned just by making you think so."

"Most people are imprisoned that way. Some like it. Back-in-the-womb predicament. What I have in mind here is that we are guinea pigs. If the mental persuasion fails to keep us in, then the opposition will use solid means, and once they have to go strong-arm, then nothing's barred."

"What are you talking about?"

"I'm thinking. I'm sure this is a probe for an invasion. There is no other possible purpose for these events. It's an investigation into what sort of people are here, what they do if disturbed and the findings are read off on computers. Then an attack would be mounted only after a great friendly infiltration. This is the invisible Fifth Column."

"There is nothing new. Wooden horses, columns of numbers, dream capsules, plain bangs on the head when they let you get near enough. By this, you reckon they think in human terms?"

"In human terms, they don't think as such, but they aggravate themselves in human ways."

The station commander spoke to someone near him, then came back.

"More signals have just come in. Routine. But they have a smell about them. I have a suspicion these are copied from earlier ones. The computer says they are genuine, but we know a thing about that computer, too. What's going to be done about this soft approach? We have nothing to get hold of. At least your Trojans had a wooden horse to look at—"

At that point the phone went dead but came live again after a half minute.

"This line is going to break," the officer said. "Look, I've got a party here of four women, one man, two due to come, and one small boy. The wall tricks seem a warning that we are not wanted to leave here and might trip up if we do. I'll hold the people here and you—"

The hot line froze. The officer waited, listening, but there was no further life to be heard.

He went back into the hall. A warm discussion stopped abruptly when he appeared.

Eight

1

They were lying weirdly on the roof. They could hear gurgling of liquid sloshing in the tank and in the engine.

There was also a sound of crumbling rock from the other side of the roof panel.

"Whatever else, don't bloody move!" Arthur hissed.

"Are you all right?"

"What the hell does that matter? We're upside down, balancing on a ledge twenty feet down a cliff and a bloody great drop below. To add to the excitement, the ledge is crumbling away under the weight and if we move we'll roll off."

"I must have lit out," Leo said. "Clumped my head on the roof."

"Pity you didn't clump it before you got near the cliff. Don't move!"

The crushing of the ledge sounded like somebody twisting a wicker basket, but then there began a series of small bumps and clops of stones breaking off and running away down the cliff face to the beach below.

Arthur remembered the rocks down there and wished he dared move an arm to wipe sweat from his eyes.

"I don't understand; we hadn't turned," Leo half whispered.

"Oh, shut up. Think. We're upside down and about to fall off. Can you think of anything? And don't think of getting out of the window. The second you start to shift the balance we'll all go."

"It's moving," said Leo. "The car. It's moving. I can feel it. Trying to roll off."

"The last thing I need is a bloody running commentary," Arthur hissed. "What was that one which went, 'If I should die before I wake, I pray the lord my soul to take—'? I couldn't pray now. Not after all these years of taking no notice. I never did believe that cod about the prodigal son—"

The crushing and cracking under the roof was getting louder, more rapid, as if disintegration was well under way.

They lay still on the inside of the ledge, all available weight trying to keep the car from rolling off.

"Are you seeing your past life?" Leo breathed. "I'm just thinking what I didn't do today. I wonder if Millie will ring that rep? About the Karsen book?"

"I don't give a tiny bugger about any book or my past life. I'm just working out what I'm going to do when I get out of here."

"What?"

"I'm thinking of the best way to murder you. This bloody ledge is going any minute now. I wonder if she can hold on somehow? Oh Christ, here it goes!"

They moved, trying to get right against the windows in the last hope of holding the balance, but it was mostly an automatic desire to get as far away from disaster as possible.

There was a weird lifting sensation, as if they were being pressed down through the roof, and then the car rolled over again and there was a great bang, as the wheels hit the ground. They were thrown about inside the body as the springs tried to take the shock. Then quiet came.

Leo hissed. "God! Arthur! Are you—?"

"I'm alive." Arthur got to his knees on the floor and peered out of the window on one side, then the other. "Where are you?"

"Stuck under the bloody pedals - my face—"

"Don't hurry. Take it easy," said Arthur, staring round the moonlit scene. "I prayed the lord my soul to take, but he didn't want it. Do you know what? He's chucked us back on top again!"

The struggle on the floor stopped.

"*What?*"

"Back on top of the bloody cliff! I can see the skid marks where we went over. Oh, my God, I am sorry I didn't go and pray every Sunday. It isn't heaven. There's the house and the church tower— Listen! That's the clock! Can you hear?"

"Give me a hand. I can't find how I got stuck down here."

"I can't find how we got back up here. Hang on. I'll get out."

It took a while to get out because the body was partly

squashed and the doors would not open, being bent into position.

"It's the seat," Leo said from the shadows below. "It's slid and trapped me. Can you get it back?"

Arthur crashed a back door open by lying on the floor and jumping it horizontally with both feet. The rest of the window burst into fragments when he did it.

It took quite a while to get the front seat back with the doors jammed and in that time the church clock clanged its cracked note twice.

"God's teeth!" gasped Leo, when he was outside and upright. "We must be the luckiest!"

Arthur went to the edge of the cliff and looked down to the ledge below. Leo joined him, turning his head to try and ease the pain in his neck. When he looked down he stopped trying.

"Jesus Christ!" he said.

"Who else?" said Arthur.

2

They sat or leant about in the large drawing room, on crates, against sheeted furniture which shone like icebergs in the moonlight through the tall windows.

"Could we have all the house lights off?" the officer asked. "Then we can get used to the moon. It could be an advantage. I think we may have had too much light up to now."

"I can't believe it," Mrs. Trelawney said. "An invasion? Right in our bay? How long have they been there?"

"Roughly forty-eight hours."

Susan went out and turned off lights, then listened at the foot of the stairs for sounds of Gawain, but there was nothing. Of all the people concerned, Gawain was the only one who felt no nervous tremors at all.

"Mrs. Elton," said the officer, "is, as you know, a writer on early civilisations, and she is quite sure that this is a repetition of what happened about seven thousand years ago. There is evidence which seems to bear that out. You've all seen the effigy, and you know now how it came here. The situation at this moment is that there are several psychological tricks arranged round us which indicate that though we may not be surrounded at the moment, we shall be if we try to leave here. The phone, as you already know, has been shunted so it reaches only the Air Force station over the river, and that has broken down temporarily, probably because it was only a rushed job of a hook-up at the start."

"Do you mean we have no means of—" began Trelawney.

"Not at present."

"Don't worry, Meg," said Watts, patting her arm. "There are plenty of us."

"I don't wish to seem daft," said Rowena, "but as this is hoped to turn out as a meeting, I don't think she should be shut up in a cupboard. She could be the introduction."

"The fertility Fräulein?" asked Elfrida, and nodded. "You could be right. Yes, a prominent place amongst us, and then if anyone does drop in, they might see our acceptance. Yes, I agree."

"How can it make any difference?" asked Trelawney. "Shut in here with no lights, one imagines all sorts of things, I mean—"

"We have no choice, dear," said Watts soothingly. "I don't really want to try that running and standing still business again. I thought I was going mad."

"I suppose the reason why people say '*going* mad' instead of just 'mad' is to impress it on the public that they are normally sane," said Elfrida. "But is anyone? I have a hate. A life-long hate about nothing. About a name that isn't a name. I'm not Elfrida. I chose that because I couldn't stand my own. Effie, Effie. In my teens I got so mad I would shout, 'Effie what?' and get shut in my room. Then when I went further I shouted, 'And Effie you, too!' and got six whacks across the bum for insolence, impertinence, indecency, lasciviousness, blasphemy and lust. But, you see, the whole creation of that fury was born of nothing at all, because I might have liked Effie— Where did I start?"

She watched Rowena go out to fetch the model woman and thought, and Gawain will suffer like me, too, poor little sod. Why pick a name like that for him? Why not go the whole hog and call him Gawain Lancelot Carados Guinevere-James? He'll hit them with a round table when he grows up. Or perhaps it's his father's revenge for Leofric. You get one flatulent name and the others bubble up like frog-spawn.

She realised the room was silent, as if everyone was listening for something.

"Well, I don't mind, of course; if all you can stick it out so can I, and if it benefits the public, so much the better, incidentally—" Trelawney said, fading in uncertainty.

"We're all talking to keep the devil away," said Elfrida.

"But if we want him to come in, what are we supposed to do?" said Trelawney.

"These people, these good people have actually had contacts with the - whatever they are," said Watts.

"And so, Mr. Watts, have I," Trelawney said proudly. "He has pawed me indecently, and what's more he wouldn't stop. I almost felt him chuckling. At my embarrassment."

There was another silence. As they watched the paths of moonlight from the windows skewing across the floor, it seemed possible for them to be suddenly peopled with the gossamer processions of Rackham's midnight fairies.

Perhaps, the officer thought, that was part of the psychological trick; bringing up the imagination to picture pitch so as to front with the images the truth of what was happening behind the scene.

"Why don't they do something?" said Susan, quickly. "Are you sure they're still here?"

Rowena came back with the model and set it carefully on top of a sheeted spinet, so that it stood in the full beam of moonlight from the middle window.

"It could almost be alive - in the moonlight," Rowena said, staring.

Trelawney bent closer to see it. "How on earth did anyone make it up in a nursery? You don't leave tools up there, do you?"

Watts said, "The bell's striking again. Is anyone up there? In the belfry?"

"That long moonbeam," said Rowena, pointing to the light path from the middle window, "is made up of fairies, all prancing about like glass moths, and coming down towards us with Titania there in the middle on a great float made of cobwebs."

"What do you mean?" asked Trelawney, alarmed.

"I don't know. When I was a child fairies always made me cuddle up and feel randy."

"You should extend that proposition in daylight," said Elfrida. "You're right. That little lady does look alive."

"If you look at one thing long enough," said the officer, "it'll move."

"Sure?" asked Susan.

"Bloody certain," said the officer, staring out into the moonlit hall.

Another silence.

"This is like a ghost watch," said Watts.

"Have you ever?" asked Susan.

"Once. I watched until my fortitude ran out of the bottom of my trousers then I bunked."

"Was there one?" asked Susan.

"We watched for something to happen," the councillor said. "And when nothing happens in an empty house one gradually becomes aware that everything is happening all round. Motes of dust in the moonbeam, bits of wood, floor joists, brickwork, plaster, ceiling beams, everything is full of life and moving and chittering and whispering as if you were in the middle of a vast open spider's hive."

"A spider's hive?" asked Trelawney.

"That is exactly what he's talking about," said the officer.

"I don't understand," said Trelawney.

"Understanding is a matter of a brain flicking an idea to another, which immediately bursts into stars of imagination that never occurred in that way before," the officer said. "It is not a matter of processing the words 'I like you' into the elements of grammar, of English, Latin, Greek, German; they are the kickers which have to be laid so that imagination may not be bogged down by a lack of discipline.

"I look at you. I don't care what you wear; only why you wanted it. I don't bother with your hair; that is an experiment with time. I don't analyse when I meet you. I *feel*. That is all. That is what you do to me; make me feel. Then if you can, say, throw me the idea that bursts in my mind like a firework, you are part of the gift of life to me."

Trelawney watched him, for a moment. "I am only a very simple woman. There is not a spider's hive."

"There is now," the officer said.

The church clock struck again.

"I feel I should be angry," said Trelawney.

"Then blow," said Elfrida. "But don't make it noisy. There may be something we want to hear."

Silence again.

"Why do you feel so sure they'll come?" Susan asked, too quietly.

"Because they have to," the officer said. "There is no point in what they have done if they don't consolidate, and that must be tonight."

"And here?" said Rowena.

"Yes, here."

"Why here?"

The officer stared at the plasticine figure on the spinet.

"I could say I couldn't tell you," he said. "That would excuse me officially. But the fact is, I don't know, but I am sure."

Silence.

"I'm getting terribly excited," Elfrida said.

"That is the trouble," the officer said. "We shall start to imagine things happening and a great tent of spiders' hives will blunt our senses. Then, when it happens, we'll see something else and not what matters."

"Each tell the story of our lives in one minute," said Rowena. "If it takes longer, you're out."

"One minute?" said Susan.

"What more is there?" Watts said surprisingly. "I was the oldest of seven. I was brought up to be a builder and assume my father's job. My father taught me to work, cut bricks, wood, pipes, stone and to cost work. My mother taught me to dress and go to church on Sundays and suffer my brothers and sisters because I was the oldest. My parents made me run, play football, cricket and jump and swim to prevent me thinking about sex. I was fed good plain food and thanked God every time, sick or not. I married the first girl I went out with and couldn't get rid of. She didn't like fucking. We have no children and no purpose in living together. I took my father's firm and kept it working. I made the secretary my mistress until she decided she didn't like it either. My brothers and sisters all went away. My parents died. They left me the eternal blessing of wondering what the hell I am supposed to be."

"But, your work on the council!" said Trelawney, in protest. "You benefit others—"

"I am on the council because my father was on the council."

"But you must have some wish to fulfil?" she asked, almost hopelessly.

"It's gone."

"The punch line," murmured the officer, watching the moonlight in the hall.

"You win," said Elfrida. "Mr. Watts, you must win with that. I want to cry."

"I've always wanted to cry," said Watts, and looked out of the window.

"I hope we are not going to have a session of telling the truth," said Susan. "Anybody else going to go?"

"Meg will have a go," said Watts. "That's fair."

"Fair?" said Trelawney, but not with much spirit. "Do you know, that thing mesmerises me. You are right. It does look - well, like a little person. It's the light, I know. I remember once in Belize—"

"No off cuts," said Watts. "Tell your story or you lose."

"I refuse to lose!"

"Start then. One minute!"

"Don't hold your watch under my nose! I have no intention—"

"Then you lose. You're out!"

"I refuse to be out just like that!"

How on earth did I think of this after all those years? Rowena thought; I must be going back to my schooldays, squatting round the dormitory floor in the moonlight—

"I am the daughter of my father's best friend," said Trelawney.

"No, no, Meg! Don't—"

"How?" asked Susan.

"When my mother told me I brought up my rhubarb tart. I never could hold custard since. I should have hated my mother but I hated my father instead, for being such a dolt. She was trying to put me off running away with my lover. My father went insane finding I was not a virgin, and beat me and shouted that he had married a nest of whores. I ran off with my man, married him, we had five children and love them all. He did his job. I did mine. The children married and went away. I see them and their children. It makes me happy, then sad. I see my mother occasionally. She is eighty and still flirts with men. I do public work because I want something to do that isn't me all the time. What am I supposed to be? I don't know. And so long as I don't have to try and find out, thanks."

She put a hand to her bosom and laughed.

"Meg," said Watts, putting his arm to her waist.

She stopped him with a hand, and suddenly there was silence again.

"Don't keep listening," Elfrida said sharply. "You'll hear yourself screaming."

"It's time the men were back from the pub," Rowena said.

"The state they were in when they went, it's

early yet," said Susan. "I'll look in on Gaw."

I am a mama rook and I go Gaw, Elfrida thought. What a bloody name for a child.

"I could swear that doll moved," said Trelawney, staring towards the spinet.

"I told you," said the officer, warning. "Don't stare at it."

"It's a strain, this waiting," Elfrida said. There is, of course, the game, but there must be something in the air to let a couple of strangers just let off their secret humiliations like those two did, and I'm not sure we ought to go on with it. I'll use it in a play, but in this setting things could get out of hand.

"How does the church clock keep striking?" asked Watts, listening to another single chime. "It hasn't been wound for years."

"Shall I get some—?" Rowena began.

"Look, let me have another go," said Elfrida sharply. "It worked last night. They know me, if they know anybody."

"Outside?" the officer said.

"Yes. I mean, it's better than just waiting. That strings you up so."

"Well, she did do it before," said Susan. "And what are we really waiting for? To make contact and find what all this is about before—"

Before the story gets around and the value of the property goes through the floor and we're left with no investment and a haunted barn we want to get out of. Yes, let her have a go, the sexy cow. If she can't fetch 'em then we've got this idea all wrong.

"What were you thinking, Sue?" said Rowena,

watching. "That she should? Because the quicker we can sort this visit out, the quicker the house will be free of it. Not *it*, exactly, but the idea that – well, what else is there? We can't just sit around all night and it might not come."

"Right," the officer said. "Please stay in here. I'll come out with you, Mrs. Elton, because the right place must be chosen so that it isn't out of sight in case of anything going wrong. You do understand that?" When she nodded, he went on, "Once we've set the ground, I'll leave you and come back to the others. Is that what you want?"

"Yes. After all, I can shout, can't I?"

I hope so, the officer thought; though sometimes the vocal chords freeze up and not much noise goes forth.

They went out, through the hall and into the bright moonlight. Once there, she stopped on the grass and turned to him.

"It has a very odd atmosphere, this whole business," she said. "Do you notice that?"

"It's been puzzling me all along. And I have an idea, though it may seem complicated.

"But consider: a woman suddenly feels someone stroking her affectionately and, looking round, finds nobody there. Am I right in thinking a normal woman would do one of two things: imagine an invisible man and scream her head off, or think she had better see a doctor about some sensory illusions?"

"Well, almost," Elfrida said, and smiled. "It depends on the character, but in general, yes, certainly."

"In this case it doesn't happen. There is no alarm.

Instead, it's more like a furtive slap and a whisper, 'Stop it, George, not here!'"

"That's what happened to the councillor. Yes. As far as I was concerned, I have had an apprenticeship of odd feelings and witch doctor's potions, mesmerism and so forth, and so, first, I was interested and then rather enjoyed it."

"You weren't frightened?"

"No. That is the point, isn't it? The finger on the back of the neck just wasn't there. The whole feeling was – well, loving, I suppose. Yes, that would be the word, now I come to sort it out into words."

"Right. But today we have two optical illusions intended to frighten and confuse: the tree and the wall. And, further, two sensory illusions; at the wall and on the church path. None of that was loving. They were more a reminder that a master was in control. And yet, so far, everybody is excited, tense, expectant and all the rest of it, but nobody is frightened. That's the thing that I can't understand."

"How is it they're not frightened?

"I believe the key to this puzzle is in the little boy, but *how* beats me. Children often see what we get blind to, or what their fresh vision sees in a different way. It might be that, but somehow I think it's something more. It's possible that the truth of this business is clearly visible, and he can see it. So can we, but we don't interpret it in the right way. The human thing lacking is fear. Could it be that something is in the air which tells us we needn't be afraid and we just accept the message without caring where it comes from?"

She looked towards the church.

"Are you superstitious?" she said.

"No. Who is?" He put a hand in his pocket and took something out. It was a small wooden mouse sitting up enquiringly on the palm of his hand. It was battered and had lost one leather ear. "I never took up an aircraft without Wilfred in my pocket and, this morning, I took it out of my kit and put it in my pocket again."

She took it, held it in her hand and turned to the church again.

"They have come back here because of *that*. The church," she said.

"Not because it has been abandoned, sold to Mammon?"

"No. Churches are often built on churches built on churches. In many cases the original church has been lost, but the reason why the spot was first chosen and then used over and over again is because the spot was chosen first as a place of maximum earth power. A crossing of ley lines, a junction of forces which primitive people could sense, and which an advanced alien, depending on natural forces for navigation aids and setting up camp, would develop and use. I think that is why they have come back to this place."

She turned and gave him his mouse. "I could feel your force in that mouse," she said. "It was odd."

"Bad?" he said.

"No. Very unusual. Very." She looked at him with her head on one side. "Well, shall I begin? Or do you think our practical talk might have broken the charm?"

"If we could tell why nobody is frightened, then we

would have broken it." He looked around. It was very quiet.

"I wonder what they look like?" she said, undoing her shirt.

"If your story of them coming to steal the women long ago is on track, then they can't be very different from us."

"But hands, hands," she said, unbuttoning the sleeves. "How did they make that model?"

"Won't this wondering put you off the mood of relaxation?"

"It's not relaxation that makes me dance. It's sheer wild excitement about nothing."

3

They went slowly back over the soft turf of the headland, down towards the wood showing above the wall they should have turned along. Leo shambled, his left leg hard to lift from the ground.

"It's not broken, is it?" Arthur asked, as they stopped.

"I'm walking, you twit."

"But not well. A chap I knew broke his neck and spent all weekend at home doing the usual things and all he felt was a headache. When he went to the doc to complain he was stuffed into plaster for months."

Leo leant against his partner and felt his leg gingerly.

"Give it a bloody good yank," said Arthur, kindly.

"No good being fussy. It might be still sticking together from congealed blood."

"Sod off," said Leo. "It's not bust. I can't feel anything."

"You can't tell yourself," said Arthur. "Like smelly breath. You have to get a friend to hold his nose when you recite the Lord's Prayer. Let me have a grip."

Arthur bent and felt the leg while Leo held his shoulder for balance.

"I don't think it's bust, but you've got a bloody great lump above the ankle. You'd better lean on me, as if you haven't for years."

"I should have stifled you years ago."

"You nearly succeeded just now. That will suffice. I won't kill you till you're better. Put your arm round my shoulders. No, not that way, you twit! That's the wrong side. You want to keep that foot off the ground in case there are bits of bone jolting about inside. I don't like the rattling. That's it. Right?"

They did a three-legged man down through the gorse-lined path.

"What do we do if there's no gate here either?" Leo asked when they were near the wall.

"Is it hurting?"

"Like buggery. I think I have done something to it. Perhaps I shouldn't have walked on it."

They got to the wall. Leo leant against it. Arthur looked down at Leo's leg as if considering whether to buy it.

"This looks about as far as you go," Arthur said. "Still, you're lucky to be alive, you murderous sod."

Leo tried to make himself comfortable against the

wall, keeping just a toe in contact with the ground on his left and leaning hard on his right leg.

"We were both in a state of moderate pissation," he said, "but after the gates being blocked I was wide awake and I did not come to the end of the wall when I was driving. And I was waiting for it! You don't think the phantom burglar-sculptor has been busy building up the walls, do you?"

"The wall ended where it should have done and then you went out over the common, straight to the cliff where we fell over. I thought you were trying one of your funny Look-no-Hands routines, and I thought you went too far."

"I was still driving along by the wall. I didn't see the cliff at all."

"You're delirious. I tell you what. You lie on the grass and I'll nip over the wall and rouse the inmates. The one thing I can't stand is when you get hurt and both the bloody women make a fuss of you."

"And you!"

"That's my entitlement. I'll give you a hand to lie down. The leg might break off altogether if you try and go down by yourself, and that sort of suppurating mess and bits of bones makes me spew."

"Leave me. I'll be all right."

"I care not whether you'll be all right or not," said Arthur, searching his pockets for a cigar. "All I am preserving is my reputation as a caring individual to the outside world. To be clobbered for leaving you to the wolves is bad for business, and might put me in wrong with the women—"

He broke off and looked one way and the other along the wall.

"I must have lost my cigar case in the accident," he said, in an unusually absent tone. "We are just about where there should be the door into our property, yet I see no door as there are no gates further back. . ."

"There is no door there now. Shut up, and go and fetch a car or something. I can't lie here all night."

"You can," said Arthur. "Now you saw a continuous wall. I saw there wasn't one. We both saw the gates bricked up. And here's the door bricked up, or somewhere here. Now you can't see it and I can't see it, but supposing it is still here?"

"Oh Christ, now we're getting on to the bald stakes," Leo said. "I see, I hear, I feel, I smell, therefore I am. Well, supposing I'm not? Suppose we didn't come back up over the cliff after all? Suppose the roll up-and-over was just a continuity scene shoved in to make us think we're still alive? Thought of that?"

"You don't get to heaven with a broken leg. And in hell they'd have burnt it off by now to isolate the pain. I'm sure it's here—" He pushed the brick wall, shook his head, moved on and pushed again further on.

Leo sat up and pulled his trouser leg.

"It's a hell of a lump," he said.

"You deserve the best of everything," said Arthur. "No, I can't find it. I'll get over the top and petty cash can buy me a new jacket in the morning."

He took the jacket off, folded it and slung it across the glass-laid top of the wall, keeping a hold on the tail end.

At that moment someone on the other side jerked it out of his grip and over out of sight.

His fury ignoring caution, he reached up, caught the edge of the wall top and tried to haul himself up to see over. He could find no hold for his feet and, while kicking to get one, he kicked the door.

4

"I must say I feel a little uneasy when he's not with us," Trelawney said. "He does seem to know what he's doing, or he can persuade us he does. What are we to expect? Apart from the church, which was a little frightening or, rather, it made one frightened of one's own brain, I suppose, which is different—"

"The officer is naturally informed of matters which he cannot pass on," said Watts, gravely.

"I understand that. Otherwise the affair sounds like a quirky joke. Are we - do you really think," she looked earnestly at Rowena, "we are in some particular danger?"

"We'd all like to know that," said Rowena. "I'm sure it is an invasion from a different world, but they might not be a murderous lot. They might be highly-developed, civilised - well, not civilised, but gentle."

"We know they have been about the house nearly a day and all that's happened has been - well, a bit silly, as far as I can make out. Something's been playing with my little boy and, of course, he likes it. They're friends now."

"But what about this - er - molesting?" asked

Trelawney. "It seemed to be a most comprehensive advance on someone's part."

"Elfrida had it," Susan said. "But we haven't. The only real and solid bit of strangery is that little figure. Why suddenly the creature decided to make it to please the boy, out of his toy stuff, and of course the fact that it is almost an exact replica of something found after seven millenniums or whatever they are."

"If we are to talk about whether there is something here or not," said Watts, "then may I say I'm sure there is. I've never spoken like I did just now, and had no intention of ever speaking like it."

"It went down well," said Trelawney, looking at him. "Don't worry. I did the same thing. It just sort of streamed. As if somebody pushed my switch and out it came. And I don't wish I hadn't. That's what staggers me. I even feel it did me good."

She looked round to the window. "She dances beautifully," she said, surprised.

"Her mum sent her to ballet school. She can't get it out of her system," said Susan. "She does that in the middle of the jungle. It petrifies snakes."

Watts felt his binoculars weighing heavy in his jacket pocket.

"She is very beautiful," he said. "But I can't really get the idea it'll charm the invaders to appear. Do you mean to say it happened last night?"

"Something happened," Rowena said. "But you'd better ask her. I think she left a lot out."

Susan went out to the foot of the stairs and listened. She heard nothing but went up and looked into the nursery. Gawain was fast asleep. In the soft light of the nursery lamp she saw there was nothing near him but teddy. She went downstairs again.

5

The bell began to crash out madly. The officer stopped in the act of helping her on with the shirt. She looked towards the tower.

"What's happened now?" she said. "It's not me, is it?"

"No. Something's in that church. I'll take a look. Who's got the key?" He helped her scramble into her clothes while the bell tolled in a kind of hiccupping session.

Then it stopped.

They went back into the house. The others had come out into the hall, alarmed by the antics of the bell.

"I must go into the church," the officer said. "And one other person to come with me, keeping well back. In this case, since we don't know for certain what's going on, it's important that, if anything happens to me, there should be someone who will see it and be able to report exactly what it was, otherwise the exercise could be useless."

"We should all go!" said Trelawney. "Do we agree?" She looked round.

"I can't go," said Susan. "But I'm all right alone. Don't fuss."

"And I'll stay with you," Rowena said. "The rest go."

"Right. Where's the key?" said the officer.

The key was fetched. Rowena also fetched the camera.

"It might be useful," she said, offering it.

"I'll take it," Elfrida said. "I've shot into tiger's mouths, or I've felt like it, anyway."

"We have to go in through a door," the officer said. "I go first. Mrs. Elton, a sensible distance behind. Mrs. Trelawney, close behind Mrs. Elton; Mr. Watts, you are the rearguard. Eyes open all round and shout if there is anything dead wrong. Right?"

They went off down the path into the gardens.

"You know, he's very good," said Rowena. "I know it's his job, but he seems to be the only one of us who isn't edging a bit into frilly-frilly land. Do you know what I mean?"

"I think you mean your inhibitions have got loose. That's what's the matter with everybody here. Those two, telling All, quite suddenly. Strangers. The queer thing is *I* felt better when they'd done it. I felt better because they felt better. I knew it. It's really very odd."

"It's nothing to do with invasion, menace or anything. It's quite different. I think there are two things happening. But don't ask me to explain what."

Susan went to the stair bottom and listened again. She turned back.

"Do you think they're *still* down at the pub?" she said. "Or has something happened?"

"How could it, Sue? There isn't room! Thirty yards to the front gate—"

"Which he said isn't there now. Still, it isn't that late yet. I mean, the gate *has* to be there. You can't vanish *holes,* can you?"

They went into the drawing room again.

Nine

1

Arthur felt all over the painted, uneven face of the door.

"It's here!" he said. "If I shut my eyes it's here!"

"God's teeth!" groaned Leo, holding his upper leg to try to stop pain. "Well, shut your eyes again and find the bloody key!"

Arthur opened his eyes and stood back.

"Hell! We haven't got it, have we?" he asked.

"Why don't you go back to the wagon and get the sacks out of the back, then put them on the wall and get over?"

"They've already got my coat." Arthur pushed his hat back on his head. "Good God! I've still got my hat on!"

"Triumph for civilisation!" said Leo. "He's got his hat. He can still look like Humphrey Bogart! Look, get the sacks and this time hold on with both hands. Try one first, then sling the others over quick, and keep holding on."

"It all sounds easy when they tell you how to do

crêpes suzette on the television, so why do I set fire to the kitchen every time?" Arthur said, as he trudged away up the path through the gorse. He came back quickly. "There's a frigate out on the bay, steaming about in all directions."

"Hooray, the cavalry's arrived! Succour for the suckers. Get over the bloody wall and do something. I'm almost fainting with the pain."

"Why don't you? It would stop all this distracting yowl." Arthur slung a sack on top of the wall and held on, fingers clenched. Nothing happened. He slung two more, holding the ends fast. After a moment he said, "Right. You, too, can be an acrobat," he said, grabbing the top of the wall. "With our new pliable reinforced steel ball box and hernia holder—" He heaved himself up until he was lying on the wall top on his belly. "God! This is ruining my digestion! Do you realise I'm doing this for spurious love of a friend? Or the peace of his wife, and spell it your way. Goodbye!"

He went over the wall, legs flying. There was a muffled thump and crushing of vegetation.

"Bloody fool," Leo said quietly, then called, "are you all right?"

"I wasn't when I started. What the hell I'm like now I hesitate to feel."

"Hurry up, man!"

"Hurry up, my arse! I've landed in a blackberry bush. When I get there I'm going to have a large scotch and a cigar. Then I'll tell them where you are—" There was a screech of tearing and a thumping and crushing of twigs, then a muffled voice, "tell them back home I tore my balls off for the sake of a friend. Oh

Christ, now I've hit a tree! I can't see under this bloody wall! Oh shit!"

There was an abrupt quiet.

"What's happened?" Leo called.

There was no answer.

"Arthur! Are you all right?"

The silence seemed to be gathering a density, like something growing all round him, damping out all noise. He could feel it surrounding him, growing into a pressure in his ears. He struggled into a sitting position and looked all round. Everything was still under the motionless moon. Still, as if it had died; like a film stopped.

"Arthur!" he shouted. "*Arthur*!"

His voice sounded in his ears like someone shouting from miles away, feeble, unintelligible, like some meaningless whisper on the wind.

Yet from somewhere he could hear the humming engines of the frigate in the bay, clear in the still night.

2

"We were talking about these, well, invaders," Rowena said, "and one thing he said was he thought they used a sort of sense extension to feel things a good way off from them, you know, sort of electronic feelers coming on radio waves of some sort."

"I suppose there are ways of doing that," Susan said. "Bit voyeur, though. Enjoying yourself without being there."

"Suppose it isn't used for that," Rowena said. "I

know the women said it felt like that, but it was when the fat lady used the key word "comprehensive" that I thought it might be a sort of scanning, finding out shape, like they do bumps on ocean beds."

Susan sat on a crate and looked at the floor.

"Well, it could be," she said. "But there are so many things it could be. And the real point is, why did it happen only to Elfrida? Effie!" she laughed a moment, "- think of that, poor soul! - Elfrida and the councillor woman?"

"Well, now, children," Rowena said, looking at the little figure on the spinet, "I thought it might happen when somebody got really engrossed in looking at Little Lucy there. Elfrida was, she says last night, and the councillor couldn't take her eyes off."

Susan looked up with an odd expression.

"And Elfrida, of course, threw herself double breasted into the game, and the people sort of put her in a radio trance and took her off for a closer examination. Urgh! Anyhow, she says she was surrounded by cubish people, but supposing they were off-Earth computers, flicking questions and taping them up?"

"She thought they were alive, but I must say when I see those terrible little metal things humming away and flicking lights and spinning things back and forth as if they can't make up their minds, I get so I half expect them to start walking about and shoving me out of the way."

"Then, you see," Susan said, growing excited, "the figure could have been made by this radio touching in the playroom, without anybody being there. And it wouldn't have used tools, either!"

"Then if it could do that, it wouldn't have any difficulty lifting Gawain up a tree."

"That was the first thing I thought of. It was that which made me wonder when you said about this distant feel sort of thing. But he keeps saying that he has a friend, though I know he's making up what he looks like. Each time that's different, you see. Red hair, yellow hair—"

"Then maybe the true hair is the colour he *doesn't* say," said Rowena, "or maybe the kid hasn't got any hair at all and then—"

"What's the matter?" Susan said sharply. "Why did you stop?"

"It's all right. Something struck me. If we want to know what shape something is, we scan it so we can see. We send a camera somehow. We make a picture. Why don't they?"

"Perhaps they can't see!"

"If they're invisible, they wouldn't need to, would they?"

"And they wouldn't need to send invisible radio feelers, either."

Rowena flattened. "No." Then she recovered her excitement. "Sue, you sit there and promise you won't go."

"Of course I won't go. Why?"

"I'm going to try something, just to see. I'm going to concentrate on Lucy and see if I get mauled."

"Ro!"

"Sit down. Shut up. Don't frighten me. Just watch and if I start going anywhere, grab hold."

3

The officer came to the church door, stopped and looked round. Elfrida stood on the first step up to the graveyard, Trelawney on the path behind her. At the rear stood Watts, gaunt as an undertaker, quite still, but for his head which turned slowly from one side to the other, as if he had a clockwork neck. His was the only movement to be seen under the serene moon.

The officer unlocked the door and went into the church. Diffused moonlight came through the high, stained-glass windows, laying dust beams like buttresses across the nave. It looked a vast place, the hall into another world, silent, remote. He turned towards the tower on his left. There was no sound of anyone behind him, though Elfrida was then crossing the aisle from the entrance, with Trelawney a pace or two in her rear.

He walked slowly, and stopped twice, listening and looking between the stone columns on either side of the nave. He saw moon shadows but nothing that moved. Even the motes in the moonshafts seemed to be still.

The arched doorway into the tower was clear, a cut-out in a white paper wall. He went to it and stepped through into the tower, keeping in direct line with the doorway so that he might be seen by the followers.

He heard a frightened whisper, brief and indistinct from one of the women, then silence again. He looked up into the body of the tower. Light from two small slit windows cut across the shaft of the tower, but he could see the bell beams and the iron cage of the clock mechanism high up, black against the diffused glow coming in through the louvres of the tower openings.

Everything was quite still. He began to feel disappointment. The idea that the bell chiming had been some sort of warning faded with the silence. In his theory there should have been activity when they came into the church and long before he had got so far.

Perhaps *we* don't really count, he thought; but it is we who are invaded. They wanted to overcome us, for whatever reason. So it is possible, as I hunched last night, that there is a rival incomer, and the two are eyeing each other. We haven't much to go on, but there have been signs and indications which we've got a hold on, showing that they are here. But only signs of one lot. If there is another, why haven't we got wind of them?

He looked at the outline of the ladder zigzagging up the tower into the clock room, then turned and saw the two women standing, one after the other, about twenty feet down the great avenue of the nave. Far back, it seemed, the gaunt undertaker stood, still working his clockwork head.

Good stout people. Courageous. Firm. Why undertaker? Why do I think undertaker? Edgar Allen Poe, Usher, the box of teeth and swirling lips, the undertaker, mortician, maker of peace and decency, hide it, hide it, stop the stink, the rot; don't make the worms climb out and jump, mortician, the stinking bones – but it's not bones that horrify, it's flesh, purple, rotten, suppurating, bursting-open flesh, turning slowly into life, new life, infusing the earth and the air with energy and vitality, new plants, new beauties, new mass, new generation, and if I go up that ladder I have no defence and down they come on me and harder down I go and smash into bones and burst flesh and water and mess and the undertaker will shovel me into a box and so I live again through worms and earth and stem and flower and seed and fall and rise—

"Is there anything?"

He heard the whisper from across the waves of light years. He turned and went to the heavy door and leant against the edge, looking back to the taut woman, only feet away.

"Yes," he said aloud. "There is something, but I don't know what it is." And then he realised that in country areas the builder is the undertaker, his carpenter the coffin-maker. A logical run, after all. He stood away from the door, and again looked up to the shadows of the clock cage.

Elfrida came in and looked up.

"He used a torch," she whispered, and turned. "It was on this shelf." She got it and gave it into his hand.

He stood for a few seconds looking up, then he raised the torch and shone it. There was a scurrying sound and small shadows moving up beyond the clock, then everything was still again.

"Bats," she said.

He turned off the light.

"Were they there before?"

"Well, they didn't flap then. But they wake at certain times, don't they? In Africa you get them like pterodactyls. Are you all right?"

"Yes."

"Are you *sure* there's nothing here?"

Trelawney whispered from the edge of the door opening.

"What's happening? Are you all right?"

The officer turned towards the women. "It must be a mechanical trouble," he said. "There is nothing here that can help us. I was hoping there would be."

4

The commander stared at the sheets coming out of the ship's computer.

"This is incredible," he said. "Four sweeps on same area show nothing; a fuzz; nothing; a sub; and now, on the fifth, a shifting fuzz. Our signals are being played up. but we have one definite fact; something *is* there and it's cocking up the search for it, but the cock's going soft. Get the chopper in the air. I think we have contact. But why now, not before? Why the gradual show? Is some protection gimmick dissolving down there and making an electronic strip show, you might say, Carver?"

"You might, sir, yes. But it's gone again."

Ten

1

Leo called again and heard nothing but a distant creaking and tearing of twigs. Again he felt the pressure in the air deadening his ears. Something was happening all round him but he could not see it. It was in the air, a pressure, vibration, a pulse; he could not sort out what it was. It might be coming from behind the wall, but it seemed too pervading to be coming from just one place.

He began to think in panic terms of invaders pressuring the air, holding it still, so that no one could move his limbs but was held in a straitjacket of cushions. Of people having to wait, still as statues and watch the invaders appear at last, coming up out of the sea to take their prisoners at leisure.

He turned over and came close to the wall, then got a hold on the brickwork joints. It needs repointing, he shouted in his head; we must get it repointed; value, keep the value; stop it falling down; get it done— He got up until he was on one foot and leaning against the wall. He could not feel his ankle except as a lump of lead on the end of his leg, but when he touched ground pain shot up and into his spine like a lightning flash.

He felt his face wet and cold from sweat.

"Arthur!" he called again. His voice was further away than ever.

He turned his head and looked out over the bay. The frigate was stopped on the quiet sea, a perfect model ship sitting on a pond. Like a duck snoozing. An iron duck, listening, watching, waiting for a fish.

Then he saw a difference but could not make out quite what it was. The surface of the sea was beginning to ruffle, not like being touched by some rising wind, but becoming disturbed, like the surface of water in a saucepan, on the point of simmering.

The ship moved, water frothed at the stern as she swung in an arc away from the suddenly troubled water.

The disturbance grew. It looked as if the sea was beginning to boil.

And then he realised what it had to be.

Something very big was coming up from the bottom.

Fear was coming in on him from all sides.

"Arthur!" he shouted. "Can you hear me?"

He could hardly hear his own voice now.

2

Susan took a step towards the silent girl.

"Is it happening?" she asked huskily.

"Yes. Sort of stroking. It *is* that. It is!"

She put out a hand suddenly and grabbed Susan's. "Let me get out into the hall."

They ran and stopped by the open main door.

"Are you all right?" Susan asked.

Rowena laughed breathlessly. "Sure, I'm all right. I suppose it was just having asked for it and then getting it. Well, we know one thing now. It is Lucy that does it. She must be some kind of receiver. You concentrate on her, she tips off the computers back home and out come the feeling waves."

"All this done by a lump of plasticine?" Susan said.

"No, it couldn't be, could it? Then the only other thing is the thing – person who made it must be around and sees us looking at his work and that starts the— Oh lord! that's worse!"

Susan turned and looked up the stairs.

"Did you hear anything then?"

"No."

Susan looked up again. "I think I'll just pop up."

"Yes. Yes, I'll come with you," Rowena said quickly.

As they got to the top, Rowena looked down into the hall. It looked empty, then a shadow fell across the step.

"Arthur!" Rowena said, relieved.

Arthur looked up. "God! I've got a head on me. It had a bash. Lucky I had my hat on. Softened it. I must have had a blackout just now. Don't remember actually getting here."

"Oh Arthur, you had more booze down there," Rowena said, coming downstairs.

"Only one," said Arthur. "I keep getting a sort of

thump in the ears. Oh, Leo's twisted his ankle. I want a car to fetch him, poor soul."

"A car?" said Rowena. "Where's Leo's?"

It fell over a cliff, crashed on a ledge, then got thrown up again and bust its springs and the roof's bust in, and so it is no longer fit for carriage service. "It won't go," said Arthur, believing the shorter version would be considerate.

"Take mine," said Susan in a stage whisper as she leant over the railings.

"Ta," Arthur said. "I'll take a modicum of scotch first in favour of my headache, which is pounding like the Atlantic rollers on the shores of Perranporth." He walked to the kitchen.

Rowena ran down the stairs and came up behind him.

"How did you hurt your head?"

"It's a long story, full of doubtful morals," Arthur said and turned and grasped her to him. "Darling, don't be flummoxed, but we had a slight accident, and I'm really beginning to feel I've cracked my pan. I won't take my hat off because it was on all the time and I think its full of liquid brains."

"Take it off, let me look," she said and turned to the light switch, then stopped.

A shadow cut off almost all the moonlight from the kitchen window.

"What's that?" she said.

They heard Susan running fast down the stairs to the front door.

"My God! Look! Look out here!" she yelled.

The two turned and went out into the hall.

3

As they came out of the tower door into the moonbeam buttresses of the nave, the undertaker moved more than his head. He turned and looked down towards the altar place and the crates and boxes and heaps.

"Something – down there!" he said. His voice echoed in the vast place like imps sniggering into the roof space as they grinned at the alarm below.

The officer went forward and signalled the women to stay where they were. Behind him they heard the sound of the bats scurrying in the belfry, and the bell murmuring uneasily. He went quickly towards the east end, while Watts backed, subconsiously, towards the main door.

Then suddenly, like a curtain drawn across the sky outside, the moonbeams were cut off. The officer stopped.

Trelawney shouted, "What's happening? Is everybody all right?"

The imps in the roof shouted it to each other like the volleying in a five-sided tennis game.

"Shut up!" the officer said, and went forward into the new darkness.

He could hear movements ahead of him, but they seemed to be going upwards from the floor, and then moonlight returned in part, and he realised what the shut-down might have been.

"Out!" he said. "Quickly! To me and out!"

They obeyed at once and hurried to the church door and out on to the path. There they stopped abruptly, looked up and stayed without making any sound at all.

4

Arthur leaned against the doorpost, the women just stood looking at the great aircraft which had silently arrived up over the trees of the wood and now halted over the space between the church and the vicarage.

"A flying Dover sole," said Arthur, but he did not grin. His eyes were too wide open.

The great ship shot down what looked like slanting glass bars, three to the church roof and one on the grass where Elfrida had danced.

There was no noise of engines or any movement until there was a sudden, fast little rustling noise from behind them. Only Susan looked sharply round into the hall, alarmed that it might be the child.

Instead she saw the impossible running through a shaft of moonlight from the Glory Hole window.

"My God—!" Then she covered her mouth.

The little woman ran at frantic speed out and between their legs. They saw her sprinting to the glass bar on the grass, and then shoot straight up it towards the belly of the aircraft, still moving her limbs like a small human being.

From the church they could see other small figures, like tiny monkeys, following each other up the slanting bars into the motherly belly. And as they went, the bars pulled up after them.

The bars disappeared. The great ship moved away silently out over the bay and then rose upwards and seemed to be gone beyond the moon within five seconds.

Only Susan ignored the mighty ship in her first awakening.

"She was real all the time!" she whispered. "She was *alive!*"

Arthur took off his hat at last and wiped his face with it.

"No wonder we couldn't think of the tools used to make it," he said. "That scotch. I must have that scotch, then I'll fetch Leo."

Things went slowly. The party from the church walked back like a defeated army. There was a discussion on the steps, while most eyes watched the sky without properly understanding what they were wanting to see.

"And that was Gawain's friend!" said Susan. "Fancy him making up all those lies about boys with red hair and yellow hair."

"My dear girl," said Arthur, who now had his scotch in hand, "he was keeping his girl friend secret from his Mum. That comes naturally to boys before the age of compromising ardour."

"It should have been a help in guessing what was happening," the officer said. "Children are frightened of giants. Lilliput is their world."

Trelawney said, "But have they gone? Do you think they've gone?"

"I'm sure they've gone, for the time being. A fault showed up in the ship. Previously we saw nothing, tracked nothing. This time, full view. That was one reason they went off home to work it out again."

"How did they do it first time?" Arthur said.

"I'll have a guess. An envelope of some sort of gas

that adheres to the hull in any circumstances, making it invisible by any means."

"And the sea dissolved it?" Arthur said.

"Well, the sea didn't. They would have calculated for seawater. Possibly, what they couldn't calculate for was pollution: acids, oils, effluent - you guess. They probably wouldn't have known that much about our sins."

"And just becoming visible made them go?" Elfrida looked at him curiously.

"It revealed a bad weakness, but I think there was something else. I don't know what."

"Do you think there will be another attempt?" Trelawney asked. "Should we discuss the matter in council?"

"Of course, you'll have to," Arthur said hotly. "It isn't our private affair, is it? I agree with our friend that something must have gone wrong. A real preventive turned up somewhere, otherwise the little probe would have turned into a full scale run-in. That vehicle was big enough to hold thousands, if they were all the size of little Madam Titzanbum."

"I think they came for information," the officer said, "as a preliminary to an invasion."

"I must go and fetch Leo," Susan said, suddenly. "Come and show me where he is."

She grabbed Arthur's hand and dragged him, glass and all, to her car. She shouted back over her shoulder.

"Watch for Gaw, Ro!"

Watch for Gaw Ro, Elfrida thought; what kind of fearful sound is that?

Arthur shouted over his shoulder as he remembered something.

"That outside bog's blocked up. I think there's a great wad of plasticine down the pan."

"Only Gawain uses it," said Rowena, almost to herself. "And she looked just like the stuff."

"Never invisible," said Elfrida. "Just chameleon."

5

I think I have enough to convince anybody that I have done useful work and carried out instructive experiments with human people. I have established that, by making it appear there is no hole in a wall, they accept there is no hole in the wall and they actually kid themselves they bump into it because they can see there's no hole in the wall.

They see a tree in the wrong place, look at the ground to see if it's been disturbed and leave it at that, accepting the miracle, like the holes in the walls, because they can see it.

The two men in their vehicle were so sure of their own eyes they actually went over the cliff, while thinking they must be somewhere else. I put them back on top, but think that I might be accused of negative action, as far as the experiment is concerned.

Letting people run to a corner, then lifting them and putting them back where they started is amusing rather than instructive, I find. Humans do it with insects and get the same results.

An interesting point is that both humans and Philodons were *aware* of my presence, but as I cannot be seen, heard, smelt or felt, they tried to think I was something else, or even *themselves*. I feel somewhat short in temper at the thought of being dismissed as an attack of nerves.

The one who stood out was the officer who thought his way through the tree and the wall, and even through his own unusual prowess. Unfortunately, he is not representative, because he knows very well the cause of all the miracles and has decided that I am here.

Not long ago he walked out of the house by himself and down to the tower and he looked up and almost into my face, if I'd had one, and said, "Thanks!" Then he walked a few paces away and looked back. "For everything!" he said, and went back to the house.

As for the visitors, if it hadn't been for that irritating ringing of the bell when I moved, I might not have dissolved their gas envelope and spoilt the ship's invisibility, but then I might. Wars are best put off as long as possible, and I hate them when I am on holiday.

Of course, the minute they were naked, they ran. Like a soldier in one of those iron tanks who feels like a tiger, until he sees that his iron has gone to butter, and then he feels like a sitting duck.

And that brings to me my farewell to the officer and his very pretty little ladies. I make him one more gift. He can write what I have seen, but he'll think that what I put into his head is his own guess. No worse for that. Certainly I don't want any accusations of frittering away time, writing chronicles in the drifting smuts of the universe.

Of course, I shall put forward all my notes and memos of this visit and my observations, and the Old Man will throw them all into the incinerator. He won't believe I find people down here. He usually thinks I dreamed it all up.

I can't think why he believes in God above and nothing below.